THE LOST LASS OF SHEFFIELD

VICTORIAN ROMANCE

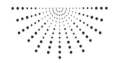

ROSIE SWAN

© 2021 PUREREAD LTD

PUREREAD.COM

CONTENTS

IN THE BEGINNING

ASHTON VILLAGE, NORTHFOLK COUNTY,
LONDON CITY, 1870

T hrough the ages, it has always been common place for loving parents to shield their children from trouble in any way they can.

On a hot summer Monday, Teresa Rider, thirty eight year old wife and mother of four sons was screaming her head off in the throes of childbirth. Her mother, Chloe Baxter, a very experienced and long term midwife was boiling water and getting ready to deliver her seventh grandchild. Chloe's brow was creased with worry because the birth of this child would either mean the mending or ending of her daughter's marriage.

Terry was a good wife and mother who had sacrificed greatly for the man she'd been married to for the past eighteen years. Her husband George was a good man who had suffered greatly and was currently handicapped, using crutches to get around.

While working at the London Docks as a loader, one of the pallets had become lose and dumped its cargo of corn flour filled barrels on George and his colleagues. He'd been seriously injured and barely escaped with his life. Chloe always termed it a miracle that her son-in-law had survived the accident while three of his colleagues had lost their lives. With a badly injured back, George was unable to work and so was laid off on medical grounds. As a casual labourer there were no benefits for him and he'd walked away penniless after serving the shipping company for over fifteen years. Unable to provide for his family, his wife Terry had to go out and find work and ended up as a housekeeper on the Cavanaugh Estate.

The Cavanaughs were the wealthiest family in Ashton Village, Northfolk County, East London. Rumour had it that Mr. Everton Cavanaugh was actually an earl but since he didn't use the title, no one put much thought to that. Still, the family was well respected because the parents were good employers and landlords. But as soon as Terry set foot into that house, her woes began.

"Oh Terry," Chloe murmured as she prepared to receive her grandchild. "You should really be praying now that you're about to put to bed."

"Mama, I am praying," Terry gasped amid the labour pangs. "One indiscretion just for my husband's sake, Mama; one mistake and my life is in chaos."

"Well child, let's not think about the worst just yet because things might just turn around for you."

"Mama, this could mean the end of my marriage and when George finds out what I did, it will just kill him. He blames himself for getting injured at work so that I have had to go and find work. He's a loving man who provided for us and never wanted me to go out and work. That's the reason why he took double shifts at the docks and no matter how much I begged him to slow down, he wouldn't listen. Overworking himself led to fatigue and that's the reason he wasn't alert when the accident happened." Terry sniffed. "When he finds out about this baby, he'll never forgive himself or me. Mama what will I do?" The cry was wrenched from her heart.

"Have this baby is what you'll do since your time is nigh and then we'll deal with the consequences thereafter. And now I want you to calm down because you're very tense and agitated and it's stopping this child from being born."

Normally, Chloe didn't like doing this work alone. She would always have someone assisting her to help in deliveries but not this time. Too much was at stake here and Ashton Village was a tiny village where rumours spread like wildfire.

"Mama, thank you for being here for me," Terry struggled to sit up when she got some respite. "I don't know what I would have done without you all these months when my head seemed like it would explode."

Chloe wiped her daughter's brow with a damp cloth. "Save your breath now for you'll soon need to bring this little one into the world."

"You're the best mother in the world and I never say that enough, Mama."

Chloe gave her daughter a tight smile. Much as she wanted to reassure her daughter that all would be well, she too was very scared. And she didn't want her daughter to sense her fear because Terry had really suffered for the past nine months. Not a single day had gone by without her daughter weeping with remorse at the one action that had given her husband his health back but had also ripped through their marriage.

And it was all because of the youngest Cavanaugh boy, who was also the Black Sheep of the family. Barely seventeen, he'd returned home from Eton after leading his classmates in a fight with another class and had been suspended. Everyone in Ashton knew that he caused trouble wherever he went and mothers cautioned their daughters against even talking to him. Even married women weren't spared his amorous advances and the employee turnover at the Cavanaugh Estate was high especially when Edgar was at home.

When he caught sight of the new housekeeper, he just wouldn't leave her alone much as she told him that she was happily married. Even though Terry was in her late thirties, she had the kind of face and childlike innocence that made her look much younger. With thick golden hair and bright grey eyes, she was a real beauty and many a man had tried to woo her but she was faithful to her husband because she loved him with all her heart.

Edgar Cavanaugh became so obsessed with Terry and tried all he could to get her to give in to his amorous advances. She resisted and begged him to leave her alone but he just wouldn't listen.

She was considering leaving her employment because he'd become such a nuisance when George had a relapse and had to go to hospital. Something had happened to the nerves in his back after the first surgery he'd undergone after the accident and he was in excruciating pain. Urgent surgery was required or else he would be dead within days and Terry had no money. All their savings had been eaten up by the earlier medical bills and she was in deep despair.

Knowing that her employers Everton and Hortensia Cavanaugh were kind people, she decided to approach them for a loan. Unfortunately Mr. and Mrs. Cavanaugh as well as their older son Hugh had travelled to Paris for their first born daughter's wedding. They wouldn't be returning for three months and George would be dead by then.

But Edgar was at home and a desperate Terry turned to him for assistance. He only had one condition after which he would give her all the money she needed.

Desperate and with nowhere else to turn, Terry gave in, got the money she needed for George's surgery and aftercare and resisted any further advances from her nemesis. But the young man seemed the more obsessed and wouldn't leave her alone. So Terry resigned from her employment at the Cavanaugh Estate, moved her family away from Ashton Village to the other side of London. In order to survive and put food on her family's table, she started taking in other people's wash.

Then just three weeks later she found out that she was with child. Under different circumstances that would have been a good thing, for she yearned for a little girl because she had four boys the last of whom was eight years old. The only problem was that she couldn't be sure if the child was her husband's or as a result of her one act of adultery with Edgar Cavanaugh.

All these thoughts were going through Chloe's mind as she walked around the small room listening to her daughter's grunts and groans.

"No one can ever know what you did, Terry," Chloe had told her daughter eight months ago when she'd come to her in a panic and confessed everything. "The baby will be born and everyone will have to believe that he or she is your husband's offspring."

"Yes Mama, but that's only if the child is born with dark hair such as George and our other sons have or have golden hair such as mine and either grey or dark eyes. But if he or she is born with red hair, green eyes and the Cavanaugh Streak, Mama, everyone will know whose child it is."

Chloe's prayer was that the soon coming baby would look like her daughter or son-in-law.

"Mama, I think the baby is coming," Terry said and ended her sentence with a loud wail.

Chloe positioned herself between her daughter's legs, years of experience telling her that even though Terry was in a lot of pain this would be an easy birth. But her mouth wouldn't stop moving in prayer. When the child's head started crowing, she let the tears fall.

Terry heard her mother's anguished sigh. "Mama what is it?"

"Red Terry, the baby's hair is red."

"Oh Mama," and the two women wept as the baby, a beautiful girl entered the world. This was Terry's only daughter and Chloe's second granddaughter because the other grandchildren from her other offspring were all boys save for one. This was Terry's daughter but Edgar Cavanaugh's too, from the bright green eyes and large dark stain on her left shoulder. This was the birthmark known by everyone in the county that proved that a child was a Cavanaugh. The first thing that husbands who suspected their wives of infidelity did when babies were born was to look for the large birthmark on the left shoulder of the newborn. Thus the innocent were vindicated while the guilty were made to suffer the consequences of falling prey to the wealth of the Cavanaugh boys, Hugh and Edgar.

"Mama, I'm so sorry," Terry wept as she looked at her new baby. She longed to nurse her but her mother was firm on that and forbade it. "I let you down when you brought me up to be a virtuous woman. Now my marriage is over and this child will be shunned and called all sorts of names."

But Chloe shook her head, "No Terry, you're a virtuous woman who was caught between a rock and a hard place and did what you could for your husband to live. George and your sons need you. It was your love for George that put you in this situation."

"Mama, please don't make excuses for me. I didn't have to succumb to that boy's advances."

"No you didn't but to save your husband's life you sacrificed your virtue. It's not your fault and I'll never think any less of you. If anything, I have learned to respect you so much," Chloe gently stroked her daughter's hair. "I may not condone infidelity but these were tough circumstances for you and I understand why you did it."

"Mama, I just wish I had died during childbirth for then I wouldn't be feeling so much anguish. I love my family and I love this child too but I know that I'm going to have to choose one."

"Listen to me Terry," Chloe cupped her daughter's face with both palms. "You will go back to your husband and tell him that the child died."

"Mama, no!"

"Yes Terry. I'm a midwife and can get you a new dead baby to take back home with you for burial because I know George will insist on seeing his child whether alive or dead."

"Mama what will happen to my daughter?"

"I'll leave London and travel to another town or village far away, probably Liverpool. There's always a high demand and need for midwives so we'll be alright. This child will survive and we'll both be fine. Meanwhile, go back and take care of your husband and sons. We may not meet again in this lifetime because it's not safe for this baby nor for you. But I promise you that I'll take good care of my grandchild. Your brothers and sisters will never know where I'm going because they know the Cavanaughs and one look at Amelia…."

"Amelia?"

Chloe nodded, "That was my mother's middle name. I will name her Amelia Jane Baxter and everyone will know that she's the daughter of my old age. Little Amy will live with me and hopefully one day you may meet again."

"Mama please just let me face the consequences and be with my little girl."

"Are you sure about all this?"

Terry nodded tiredly. "Yes Mama. This child is innocent and shouldn't have to pay for my sins." She looked down at her baby who was sleeping peacefully unaware that her arrival in the world would adversely affect her mother's and the family's lives. "Mama, is there anything to eat? I'm really hungry."

"Well, I had made some chicken broth and rice earlier. Let me just warm it for you and then I'll clean the house and washed these soiled linens." Chloe smiled as she went out to prepare a meal for her daughter which she brought back a short while later.

After eating most of the broth and rice, Terry lay down to sleep. When she woke up nearly five hours later, there was a dark haired dead baby boy lying beside her. Of her mother and newborn daughter there was no sign.

2

TOO MANY SECRETS

SHEFFIELD VILLAGE, LIVERPOOL 1877

"Amy come here at once," Chloe called out weakly from the bed. "Amy you stubborn girl, where are you?"

"Coming Mama," seven year old Amy ran into the second room of their small house. The red hair on her head was all curly and couldn't be tamed no matter what her Chloe tried to do. No number of ribbons or brushing could keep it flat and so Chloe kept it short so it could be easily combed. Amy's green eyes were bright and full of mischief and her upper lip was covered with sugar. "Mama, why are you still in bed?" She entered further into the bedroom with both hands behind her back.

"Where have you been? I've been calling you for a while."

"I was helping Mr. Pikes and Brad next door." The child spoke of their next door neighbour who was also their landlord. Peter Pikes ran a very successful bakery and had built his family a four bedroom, two story house. In Sheffield Borough of Liverpool City, he was considered a wealthy man but he was also very humble.

"Didn't I tell you not to go bothering the neighbours?"

"Mama, Brad and I were helping Mr. Pike pack the bread and buns and he gave me one to eat." She brought out her left hand from behind her back and Chloe saw the half eaten bun covered in white sugar. "Mama do you want a bite?"

"Amy listen to me," Chloe struggled to sit up. "You're now a big girl and need to pay attention to what I have to say."

"Yes Mama."

"Come closer," Chloe whispered. "Sit here on the bed next to me," her hand was thin and Amy could see the veins clearly. "Amy?"

"Yes Mama."

"You know that I love you very much," the child nodded. "But you know that I won't always be here to take care of you."

Amy stopped licking the sugar from the bun and looked up at the woman she knew to be her mother. "Why Mama, are you going somewhere?"

Chloe laughed but it turned into a coughing bout that left her quite breathless. "Water," she said hoarsely.

Amy rushed to get her mother some water and when her back was turned, Chloe spat into the piece of cloth she kept hidden under her pillow. There was much blood in her saliva and she wanted to weep as she looked around the small room.

This place had been home for them for nearly five years now and because of her friendship with Mrs. Alice Pikes, the landlord's wife, the rent was low. Consisting of two rooms one of which served as the living room and this one, it suited the two of them very well. Mr. Pikes had built her a small kitchen just outside the front door and to Chloe, this was paradise.

The small bedroom had two cots as well as a bedside table that was in between the beds. The large trunk that was under her bed was her safe where she stored their possessions and all their good clothes while the everyday ones hung from pegs driven into the wall.

She never thought about her life before coming to Liverpool because it was too painful to do so. Leaving her seven children and six grandchildren behind was more than she could bear but love had made her take the step that led them to this place. Everyone believed that she was a widow who had borne a baby in her early forties and she never once revealed to them that Amy was her granddaughter. She didn't want any loose lips divulging that information to her beloved grandchild and causing her a lot of confusion. But it seemed that she would have to reveal her secret because her body was failing her. There were too many secrets in her life which she would take to the grave with her, but not this one.

"Oh Raymond," whenever Chloe was distressed, she thought about the husband who had died suddenly and left her to bring up seven children all on her own. Life hadn't been easy for them but working as a midwife and a good one at that ensured that her family wanted for nothing. If only her husband had been alive, she wouldn't have to go through this alone.

For two years now, Chloe had known that she was very ill when she would suddenly get breathless and experience sharp chest pains. But she'd put it down to fatigue because Sheffield was a very busy town that served as the suburb of Liverpool.

The population of low income dock workers and other petty traders was high and as a midwife, Chloe delivered on average twenty to thirty babies a week. The work kept her and Amy well fed and clothed and they could afford this two roomed house in a safe neighbourhood.

She'd even started teaching Amy the trade of being a midwife.

"You never know when you'll need to help a woman who is putting to bed and it's never too early to learn such lessons, dear child," Chloe had told Amy just two months ago when she took her along to help a woman about to have a baby.

"Mama, when people are bearing children is it like when kittens are being born?"

"Where did you see kittens being born?" Chloe looked at her granddaughter in astonishment. This girl never ceased to surprise her with her quick study of the things going on around her.

"One day Brad took me to his grandmother's house before she died. I saw her Tabby cat removing small kittens from the stomach. Is that how people also have children? Do they remove them from the stomach?"

"Yes," Chloe smiled. "It's a very difficult process but there's nothing to be afraid of. All you need to do is remember that you're helping a mother bring life into the world and do your best."

"Yes Mama."

And Amy surprised her grandmother. She wasn't the least bit afraid and from that day onwards, Chloe took her to every delivery. Amy was her companion and little helper who ran errands and cleaned up when the work was done. She was a smart little girl and Chloe was proud of her.

But for how long, Chloe wondered. She was very ill and a visit to the doctor had revealed some gruesome news. Her lungs were not working properly and she didn't have long to live.

Amy brought the water and held the tumbler to Chloe's lips. "Take small sips, Mama. I'll heat the chicken soup so you can have some before you go to sleep."

"You're such a darling child," Chloe said as she lay down and closed her eyes. Sleep soon took over and when Amy brought the heated soup and tried to wake her up, she murmured that she was very tired. So Amy placed the covered dish on the small bedside table and sighed.

Her mother was very ill but she didn't want Amy to know. The sleeping woman had no idea that Amy had noticed the bloody rags that she normally hid under the pillow and Chloe would carry them to the outhouse when she thought Amy wasn't looking.

When Amy had told Brad about the bloody rags he'd told her that her mother had the disease called consumption, the same one that had killed his grandmother. And Amy believed him because she hung onto his every word.

Bradford Pikes was a very clever boy and Amy liked him very much. Ever since she could walk, she had followed him around and he had never once shouted at her to stay away. Though he was three years older than her, he was her best friend and protector.

Because of all the goodies from the bakery which his father gave him after helping out and which he would always share with her, Brad was a fat boy but no one dared tease him. All the other children in the neighbourhood were afraid of him and when he announced that he was Amy's protector, they didn't dare tease her.

Once Amy was sure that her mother was sleeping comfortably she tiptoed out of the bedroom and closed the door.

"How is your Mama?" Amy found ten year old Brad seated on their small dining table swinging his legs from front to back.

"You'll break that table and Mama will be very upset."

"Okay Amy darling," Brad drawled and she narrowed her eyes at him. "Sorry, Miss Amelia, it won't happen again," the words were spoken solemnly but he gave her a cheeky wink.

Amy giggled. "You're funny Brad."

"Can we go out to play now?"

Amy shook her head, "Mama is not well and I don't want to leave her alone."

"Can I stay here with you then?"

"Your papa said you should go back and help him with the packing. I'll come by tomorrow."

"I guess I have to go now," he jumped down from the table and straightened his large trousers. "I'll be back later to bring you some hot cross buns."

"Thank you Brad, you're really kind."

"That's because I like you very much, Amelia Jane and I promise that one day, I will marry you." And like he did every time he was leaving, he kissed his right index finger and then placed it over her small lips. "One day Amelia Jane, you'll be my wife."

"No you won't marry me," and they held hands, grinning at each other with all childlike innocence. Their friendship had started when Amy was just a year old and had started walking. Her mother had moved them into this house and the fat four year old boy had come to stare at them. A bond was forged between the red haired, green eyed little girl and dark haired and hazel eyed boy that no one could explain.

From that moment onwards, Amy had followed Brad around like a little puppy follows its master. They spent a lot of time together and as they grew, Amy thought their friendship would change with the birth of Brad's two sisters May and Naomi. But nothing of the sort happened and with each passing year they grew closer.

Every year on her birthday Brad would whisper in her ear that one more year had passed and brought them closer to the day when they would get married and live happily ever after. And Amy would giggle, her face quite red but it was all a game to her.

Brad was very responsible and as the oldest son and child of Peter and Alice Pikes, helped in the bakery and at home as well. He was the one who taught Amy how to wash dishes, clean the house and even cook. And she helped out at the bakery whenever her mother didn't need her and would bring home bread and cakes.

"Now go," Amy walked Brad to the door.

"I'll be by later in the day then."

"Thank you," and on impulse she kissed his cheek.

The ten year old boy turned a bright red and ran out of the house.

3

HIDE THE EVIDENCE

SHEFFIELD VILLAGE, LIVERPOOL, 1884

"I don't like that girl and the way she is always following Brad around," Alice Pikes was telling her husband as she served him mid morning tea. He'd just returned from the bakery because his son had arrived from London and he wanted to have a word with him. "Ever since Brad returned from school, Amy follows him around like a little puppy."

"Now, now, now, Mother, you know that those two have been friends ever since Amy could walk. Our Brad has been away for six months and those two have missed each other. There's nothing wrong with their friendship."

"Amelia Baxter is not good enough for our Brad and I want you to tell her not to come around here anymore. She's just like her mama and the last thing we want is Amy running around here with a big belly and claiming that she is carrying our grandchild."

"Mother, have you lost your mind? Lower your voice before someone overhears your cruel and unjustified remarks."

"I don't care who hears me because it's all true. Amy is a siren who is out to trap our Brad and I want you to stop her from coming here."

Fourteen year old Amy wiped the tears from her eyes as she remained hidden from view. She so badly wanted to see Brad and was hiding behind one of the curtains in the hallway. What had been a game to surprise her dear friend had turned out to be a kick in the stomach for her when she heard Mrs. Pikes speaking so badly about her.

"Mother, I don't agree with your words about our Amy. She's a good girl and her mama has raised her right. Besides that, she helps out at the bakery after school. You're misjudging her because to me she is just an innocent child who has missed her friend."

"Amy helps out at the bakery just because she's trying to impress you and when you're not looking, she'll sink her fangs into our son and ensnare him."

"Mother, Amy is only fourteen years old and still a child. Believe me when she's all grown up and if our Brad will want to marry her, I'll give them my wholehearted blessing. You also need to remember that Mrs. Chloe has been our neighbour for very many years and not once have you heard any scandal attached to her name. These are good people, Mother and I'd like you to continue treating them with kindness. I thought Mrs. Chloe was your good friend, what has gone wrong now?"

Alice Pikes snorted at her husband.

"Mother, be nice."

"I just don't want that girl spending time here when Brad is around. By all means let her come when he's in school and work in the house and bakery but not while he is here. She'll confuse him and he won't be able to concentrate on his studies. My son is going to become a very famous lawyer in the whole of England and needs to marry a woman from a good family. Not Amy because she's not good enough for Brad. My brother said once Brad finishes school, he'll become his apprentice in London. I can't wait for that time to come when Brad won't have to keep coming home and being enticed by that green eyed siren."

Amy bit back a sob and wished the Pikes would leave their living room so she could get out and go back to her own house. It was clear that she was no longer welcomed in this household which she'd always thought of as her second home.

"What are you doing skulking behind the curtains?" Brad's voice startled her and she jumped. "Amy, what's wrong?" he noticed the tears and stricken look on her face.

"Nothing," she dashed the tears away with the back of her hand, pushed him aside and ran out of the house.

Brad watched the fleeing girl, a frown on his face. What could have upset her so much? Then he became aware that his parents were talking in the next room. Just as he was about to enter and join them, he heard his mother mention Amy. So he stopped to listen to what she was saying, and his lips tightened.

"That Amy is nothing but a red headed and green eyed siren, not the kind of woman I want anywhere near my son."

"Mother I'll tell you again; Amy is only fourteen years old and she's still a child. It's not right for you to treat her so shabbily when she's been our

Bradford's best friend since they were little children. How do you think Brad will feel if he finds out that you don't like his friend anymore?"

"Brad is a child and will have to listen to my advice. I'm his mother."

Peter chuckled. "Mother just listen to yourself. Our Brad is seventeen years old and you call him a child. Amelia is only fourteen and you call her a woman. Aren't those double standards?"

"Brad is my only son and I'll do everything in my power to keep him safe by protecting him from the likes of that red headed wench."

"It's not in order for you to call other people's children such ugly names while protecting your own. Remember we too have daughters and I don't think you would like it if someone were to begin to refer to May and Naomi in such derogatory terms as you're doing to Amy."

"From the way you're defending that girl, I'm beginning to get suspicious. What's going on between you and that woman?"

"Mother that's quite enough!" Brad had never heard his father use such a harsh tone with his mother.

"Amy is like my daughter and I take exception to your unkind insinuations."

Alice snorted, "I'm not talking about that one, I mean Chloe Baxter. The way you're always defending them and going out of your way to give them handouts is quite disturbing. I'm also aware that they haven't paid rent for two months and yet you won't throw them out of our house and get a better tenant. I want you to tell me right now what's going on between you and Chloe."

"First of all, Chloe has always paid her rent on time without any delays. She's been ill for a long time but still managed to pay her rent on time. It's just that things have really been bad for them in the past two months you're talking about. I have faith that when Mrs. Chloe is up and about again, she will settle her account with us. Secondly, there's no reasoning with you when you're like this. I'm going back to the bakery."

Brad rushed out of the house when he heard his father's footsteps coming towards the hallway. He pretended to be just coming into the house as his father was leaving.

"Oh Pa, I've just returned."

"Good, I'm going to the bakery."

"You look upset, Pa. Is the work too much for you? I can come with you and help out."

Mr. Pikes ruffled his son's hair. He was proud of the young man who was now almost as tall as he was. "I could always use some help in the bakery. One of the men there is new and he's slowing things down. I miss the days when you and Amy would come by everyday to help. I should have paid you a salary to keep you."

"You and Ma sent me away to boarding school in London even when I didn't want to go."

"Son, getting a good education is important for you because it will open vast opportunities for you in the world. Things are changing and with the Industrial Revolution having changed the face of England in the last century, educated men are now taking over the country and the world. We want the best for you and you should work hard not to let your mother and I down."

"Yes Pa," Brad didn't argue with his father even though he now suspected that his mother had had another ulterior motive for insisting that he went to her brother in London and then to boarding school. She didn't like Amy anymore and had made sure that his absence kept them apart. Amy must have heard part of their conversation and that's what had really upset her.

From experience, Brad knew that Amy would need time to calm down. He would go and see her later after helping his father at the bakery.

Amy was doing the laundry when Brad finally got the chance to go and see her. He could see that her eyes were red from much weeping and he bent to help her.

"Stop," she cried out, snatching the garment he'd picked up. "Please go away."

"Amy, why are you sending me away? I'm your friend Brad, the man who cares about you."

"Please," she wiped her nose on the back of her sleeve. "I don't want your mother to come out and find you here."

Brad straightened up and looked at the young girl who was on the threshold of womanhood. His Amy, the reason he insisted on returning home in the middle of the year.

"I know you heard what my mother said and I want you to forgive her."

"But she's right you know." Amy stood up and looked at Brad, the sadness in her eyes nearly breaking his heart. "You'll soon be a very successful lawyer and me," she twisted her lips, "I'm having to drop out of school so I can take care of my Mama. What would a smart and refined lawyer want with a country bumpkin?"

"I don't like it when you look down on yourself, Amy," his voice was harsh but she merely shrugged. "We can't help what other people think about us but we can control our own reactions to their unkind words. You're a smart woman and I know that when your Mama is better, you'll go back to school. It doesn't matter how long it will take but one day, you'll also be a very smart and successful woman."

Amy smiled, "You always say such nice things."

"And I mean everyone of them. Now wipe your tears and give me another smile for I've missed seeing your lovely face."

But Amy hung her head instead.

"I'm scared, Brad," Amy whispered. "My mother is very sick and I don't want her to die."

"My Precious Amy, your mother won't die. Do you remember seven years ago when the doctor said she only had months to live? See how far she's come because she loves you and doesn't want to leave you. Your mother will be fine. Now finish up the washing while I go to the house and then I'm coming to take you somewhere so you will smile again."

"Thank you, Brad."

And as his usual practice, he kissed his right index finger then put it on Amy's lips and this time she blushed, quite aware of him as a handsome man. He was no longer the fat playful boy she'd loved as a friend, this was now a man whose presence quickened her pulse.

"My Amy, remember that in a few years' time, I will come and marry you."

"You're a funny man, Brad."

And he grinned at her, "I like that you're seeing me as a man and no longer as a boy, Amy. Now hurry and grow into a woman so we can get married."

He chuckled when he saw her red face as she bent down to hide her mortification from him.

4

HEART IN DESPAIR

ONE YEAR LATER

"**A**my, Amy," the desperate call roused her from her deep sleep and she quickly sat up. "Amy, I need you."

"Yes Mama, I'm coming," Amy slid out of bed and winced when her foot knocked against the small bedside table. She raised the wick and flooded the room with light.

"Ma, what's wrong?"

"I need you to turn me over. My left side is hurting and tired."

"I'm sorry," Amy did as bid and rapidly blinked her tears back. She didn't want to distress her mother further with her own sorrow. Her mother was in pain enough without having to see her crying. "Ma are you comfortable again?"

"Yes," Chloe smiled. She was a shadow of her former self and each time Amy looked at her, she wanted to weep. Her mother had always been a strong and independent woman who worked hard to take care of them. But now the disease that had started out as something simple and had rendered her bedridden, unable to do anything for herself.

It broke Amy's heart seeing her mother trying so hard to be strong even as her body failed her.

"I'm sorry," Chloe whispered and Amy saw the tears on her face. "My child, I'm very sorry for putting you through this."

"Ma please don't cry. I don't like seeing you upset in any way."

"You shouldn't be here taking care of a cripple like me. You have your whole world ahead of you and it isn't fair for me to continue holding you down. I've become such a burden to you."

"Mama," Amy knelt beside her bed. "You're not a burden to me at all and never will be. I love you and will take care of you until you get better." And she really meant it. The kind Mr. Pikes had given her paid employment at the bakery and that was how she was able to take care of their daily needs. It was hard work but she never once complained because she felt very lucky that she had the job.

"Child," Chloe tried to raise her hand but couldn't. The disease which the doctor had diagnosed as a problem with her lungs had progressed into a full stroke a few weeks ago and rendered her paralyzed on the right side. Her left side wasn't affected but she could barely use her good hand. "You're not cut out for this kind of life and deserve better. I think it's time I did something to take care of your future."

Amy frowned, "Mama, you're not making any sense and I don't want you to over tax yourself. You need to rest and then we'll talk some more later."

"Amy, you were only supposed to stay a little while with me," Chloe's voice dropped and Amy had to lean forward to hear her clearly. "You're now fifteen and growing up into a very beautiful girl. I can't protect you like I should and every day I get very scared that some man will take advantage of you and ruin your life."

Amy smiled at her mother, "Mama, no one is ever going to take me away from you and that's a promise. You will get better and we can then work together and once again rent the big rooms again from Mr. Pikes and be comfortable. We'll be happy again, Mama, I promise."

Chloe closed her eyes. "I'm tired," she said. "You also need to go to sleep now. Don't turn down the light because I don't want to be in darkness."

"Yes Mama," Amy said as she got back in bed and closed her eyes to try and go back to sleep. But sleep eluded her. Much as she tried to calm her mother's fears, she knew that what she said was true. From the time her chest and hips had filled out a few months ago, she'd suddenly began attracting attention from men and it made her very uncomfortable.

The only man she wanted to notice her was Bradford Pikes but it had been a full year since she'd last seen him. He no longer came home for the holidays and from snippets of conversations she'd overheard between May and Naomi, he'd finished school and was now an apprentice solicitor for his uncle and she was definitely out of his league. It was what his mother wanted and she'd finally got her wish.

Brad no longer cared about her and he'd forgotten all about her. She longed to ask his sisters for his address so she could write to him but they were like their mother and didn't think that she was good enough for Brad.

Alice was so cold towards them these days. Amy knew that they continued to live in this compound because of Mr. Pikes himself. Had matters been left to Alice, she would probably have kicked them out and sent them to the streets months ago. But she had succeeded in convincing her husband that since they were no longer able to pay rent on the larger rooms, they should be moved to a single room behind the bakery. It had previously been a storage room for the wheat flour that he used at the bakery and it was cramped up. The two beds barely fit inside but Amy and Chloe weren't complaining. It was a roof over their heads at least.

But Mrs. Pikes taunted and tormented them day and night, not giving them a break. Even though her husband insisted on providing food for them, Amy now felt uncomfortable receiving the handouts from their benefactor. Her greatest desire was to continue her mother's work but she wasn't all that qualified and none of the other midwives needed her services since they had their own helpers. It had been good money but that was now gone and all she could be was a labourer at the bakery and earn the minimum wage.

Going to the textile factories was also out because she had no one to leave her mother with. Chloe tried her best not to be burdensome but it still required much effort to take care of her. At least the bakery was close by and Mr. Pikes allowed her to keep running home every hour or so to check on her mother. But even the little money she got wasn't enough for the drugs her mother needed to get better.

"From the way you're moving around on the bed I can tell that you're troubled. What ails you, my child?"

Even though her body was failing her daily, Chloe's voice remained strong.

"Oh Mama," Amy sighed. "I'm really worried about you because I can't afford to buy you the drugs that the doctor prescribed. What I get from working at the bakery goes to pay the rent, on this room, because Mrs. Pikes insists on it. I don't want Mr. Pikes feeling that we're taking advantage of his kindness."

"I'm so sorry that you have to go through this, Amy. It's my fault for not taking care of matters before now. But have no fear, I promise to do something about it."

"Mama please don't say that. You've done your best for me all my life and now it's time for me to take care of you."

"You shouldn't have to. I have to find them and let them know about you."

"Mama you're not making any sense," Amy sat up. "Who do you have to find and why do you need to tell them about me?"

"Your…."

"My what, Ma?"

But Chloe didn't say another word. She made a funny gurgling sound in her throat and then slumped on the pillow.

"Mama, Mama," Amy scrambled out of bed and was immediately at her mother's side. She bent her head to listen to the sound of breathing but all she heard was something like a soft whistle that was fading away. "Ma," she screamed, shaking her mother. "Talk to me, Ma." But Chloe gave her one sad look and then closed her eyes. "Ma please wake up. Open your eyes."

Amy put her hand over her mother's chest to hear the thumping of her heart but all was still. She wanted to run out and find Mr. Pikes but the house was two blocks away and it was dark outside. The street lights in this part of town weren't working. Amy couldn't remember the last time they had worked and all manner of dangers lurked out there.

"Mama please," Amy was on her knees until morning when she heard Mr. Pikes hailing someone as he came to open the bakery. In her haste to get help for her mother, she forgot that she wasn't appropriately dressed and opened the door. She stepped out to speak to Mr. Pikes, only to come face to face with his wife.

"And where do you think you're going dressed up like that?"

"I'm sorry, Ma'am," tears filled Amy's eyes as she retreated into their small room and donned one of her mother's old frocks which she plucked from the peg on the wall. "Something has happened to my mother and I was going to find Mr. Pikes and ask him to come and help me."

"Dressed like you were?" Mrs. Pikes scoffed. "What kind of a person are you and what do you think you're doing? It's becoming clear to me that I'm harbouring a viper in my bosom and I need to get rid of it."

"Please, just help me."

"Get out of my sight and don't bother me," Brad's mother hissed and turned to walk away. Amy sank at the doorway tears pouring down her face. She didn't realise that Mr. and Mrs. Pikes were coming towards her.

"Mother tells me that something has happened to Mrs. Chloe."

"Yes Sir," Amy got to her feet trying so hard not to breakdown because she could see the sparks in Mrs. Pikes' eyes. "Last night Ma was talking to me and then she made a choking sound and fell silent. I've tried to wake her up but she won't open her eyes."

"Let us in," Mrs. Pikes pushed past Amy and walked to Chloe's side. She bent down and after a moment called out to her husband. "Father, you need to get in here now."

Amy was trembling as she stepped aside to let Mr. Pikes in. The couple conversed in low tones before Alice looked up. "Your mother is dead," she announced without any emotion on her face.

Amy felt the blood rushing to her ears and crumbled to the floor. When she came to it was to find that she was all alone in the small room and the door had been shut. She cast a quick glance over to her mother's bed and found it empty.

"Mama," she quickly sat up and then got off the bed. "Mama are you outside?" She walked to the door and turned the knob. It was locked and there was no key on her side. It was clear that someone had locked her inside their room.

Panic overwhelmed her and she started banging on the door. "Ma, where are you?" She was screaming and she heard the key being turned in the knob.

When the door opened, Mrs. Pikes stood there and she had an ugly expression on her face which frightened the young girl. "Where is my mother?"

"The coroner came and took her body away."

"Where have they taken my mother? I want to see my mother."

"You need to stop shouting like a shrew," Mrs. Pikes said. "My husband and two of his workers accompanied the coroner and he'll give you more news when he returns."

Amy once more felt her legs giving way and she sat at the doorway.

"Listen here," Alice leaned forward so those who were passing wouldn't hear what she was saying. "I want you gone from this place by the time I return. You're no good to me and now that your mother is dead there's no more reason for you to stay here like a charity case. My husband pitied you because of your mother but that has all ended. You'll go to the docks or factories like other young women and find work there. Stop living off other people's sweat and work for yourself. And I don't want to see you at the bakery again."

Amy bowed her head and said nothing, glad when she heard Mr. Pikes' voice.

5

AS GOOD AS IT GETS

FOUR YEARS LATER

"That's not how it's done," Mrs. Pikes snapped at Amy. "Can't you do anything right for once?" The irate woman grabbed the quilt from Amy's numb hands. "Why did I ever think that I could civilize a country bumpkin like you?"

Amy was quite used to the insults that were heaped on her head each day. Alice Pike and her daughters made no secret of the fact that they resented her being in their home. But Peter Pikes had put his foot down and insisted that Amy should live with them. This had been her life for four years ever since her mother passed away and left her destitute.

"I'm sorry," Amy whispered, rapidly blinking her tears away.

"You better prepare this room well. My Brad is coming home tomorrow and everything should be ready for him." Amy's heart leapt with joy. Finally the one person who could make things better in this house would soon be here. She made excuses for him that he was a very busy man and that was why he couldn't come home. But the time had finally come when he would come and take her away like he'd promised and she would be free of all this torment.

Mr. Pikes was a good and kind man but because he'd expanded the bakery and opened a second one, he was very busy. Being gone very early and returning late meant that he had no idea what was going on under his own roof. His wife dominated the home and in order to keep the peace, Amy rarely spoke with Mr. Pikes.

"Oh Mama," Amy murmured under her breath.

"Did you say something?"

"No Ma'am," Amy responded hastily. The last thing she wanted was another slap across her face and Alice Pikes was very generous with those. Any slight provocation and Amy would get it.

When would this suffering end, Amy wondered. Maybe Brad would arrive and see her pain and take her away from here. He'd promised to take care of her all her life and that was the only reason she put up with all the abuse from his mother for all this while.

Many times she thought of running away but remembered the promise she'd made to Brad that she would wait for him. What if she left and he came looking for her and didn't find her? Besides that, he loved his mother very much and in his eyes she could do no wrong. The only way to make Brad happy was to put up with his mother. She hoped that by working hard, she would win the approval of the woman who meant so much to the man she loved with her whole heart. But it seemed like all her efforts were in vain. Still, she held on because she trusted Brad and believed that he would make good on his promises made to her over the years.

"When you're done making up the bed and cleaning this room, come down to the kitchen and help me. I have to prepare all of Brad's favourite dishes for him."

"Yes Ma'am."

Brad had been away for the past four years and she wondered if he still thought about her. He was all she could think about each waking hour. Even in his absence she knew that she was in love with him.

Just before he'd left home for the last time, he'd taken her to the beach and that was one of the best days of her life.

"Promise me one thing, Amy," he held her hand looked deep into her eyes.

"What is it Brad?" His presence made her tremble and her legs very weak.

"Amy, you know that I have very strong feelings for you."

"Brad, you shouldn't be saying such things to me." She'd just turned fifteen and was aware of Brad like never before. He took her breath away and made her feel very strange. So she tried to pull away but Brad held on.

Brad had changed and she missed the boy that he'd once been. Playful and cheeky Brad had turned into a very serious looking man of eighteen whose intense gaze made her feel funny inside, like there were butterflies in the pit of her stomach.

"Amy, you're not going to remain a child forever. You're growing up very fast and in a year or two your body will have filled out. When that happens, many men will be attracted to you and they will brazenly approach and ask you to give up your virtue."

"What's that?" she asked him in confusion.

"That is a woman's greatest treasure that she should only share with the man who is her husband, the man who loves her with all his heart."

"If that is my greatest treasure then why should other men ask me for it?"

"Because dear girl, men have always desired what they can't have. And in many cases they may even try to take it away from you by force and without your consent. Promise me that you'll guard your virtue with your life and keep it only for me. When I return, I'll ask your mother for your hand in marriage then we'll be together forever."

"You want to marry me?" A blushing and breathless Amy had asked. Her palms were sweating and she was feeling all kinds of emotions running through her.

"Believe me Amy, if you were just a year older, I would marry you even today. Remember how I used to count every year on your birthday?" She nodded. "I meant every word that I said, but you always thought I was joking."

"Oh Brad," Amy felt weak and strong at the same time when she saw something in Brad's eyes that made her realize that their relationship had changed. No longer *were they childhood friends who played and laughed together. They were on the precipice of adulthood and emotions had changed as had their bodies.*

Brad was now tall and very broad shouldered while she was slender. When he took her in his arms she didn't resist but rested her head on his chest hearing his heart beating and knowing that this was where she wanted to be for the rest of her life.

He gently raised her chin and they shared their first kiss which shook them both. But for Amy it felt like Brad had put his mark on her and she could never belong to another man.

Now it was four years later and he was coming home. Her heart wouldn't stop pounding in anticipation of his arrival.

In his absence she kept to herself and couldn't even make friends with the neighbours because she didn't want his mother and sisters to give him a bad report about her. She also kept in mind his warning about men desiring her virtue, whatever that meant.

As soon as she was done helping out in the kitchen she took two pails and went out to the well to fetch some water. And that was the day that she finally found out what virtue meant.

When she got to the community well, she found Belinda Taylor seated on the slab on the side and she was weeping. It was the middle of the day and there was no one else in sight. At first Amy wanted to ignore Belinda because the other girl was always unkind to her especially when other girls were present. They would wait for Amy to come to the well to fetch water and then tease her mercilessly. And it was all because of the ugly mark on her left shoulder. Her mother had told her that she'd been burnt as a little girl.

It was May Pikes who had seen the mark as they were bathing together and told the others and they never gave her peace after that. From that time onwards, Amy had never exposed her body to anyone because of the shame she felt. The other girls said she was ugly and she believed them. Brad had seen the mark years ago when they were small and expressed concern, asking if it hurt.

"Belinda what's wrong?" Amy asked, feeling sorry for the other girl.

"What do you care?" Belinda snapped.

"I'm sorry that I troubled myself feeling sorry for you," Amy filled her pails with water and then prepared to leave.

"Wait," Belinda called out.

"Why? So you can insult me some more?"

Belinda covered her face with her hands. "I'm sorry for being so mean and unkind to you and yet you don't deserve it."

Amy sighed and put the pails on the ground then she went to sit next to Belinda. "Tell me what's wrong."

"I did something terrible, really terrible," Belinda sobbed. "My aunt will kill me when she finds out. What will I do?"

"Is there anything I can do to help?"

"If you had the power to turn back the clock to two months ago, that would really help."

"Belinda, I have to go back to the house because Mrs. Pikes is waiting for me. Brad is coming home tomorrow and we're getting everything ready for his arrival."

"You're lucky because he'll come and marry you. You're a virtuous woman Amy and Brad is lucky that you've been faithful and kept yourself."

"Stop crying and tell me what's wrong."

"It was Chadwick Jenner," Belinda covered her face. "He made me do it."

Amy's brow creased in a frown. "What about Chad? Didn't we bury him just last week? What did he do to you?"

"He took me to his house when his parents weren't there and told me that he loved me. That was six weeks ago. He said that if I loved him then I would be with him. I gave in and he hurt me and then chased me out of the house when it was all over," she sobbed. "He didn't care that he'd hurt me."

"I don't understand," Amy looked at her age mate in confusion.

"I lay with Chad and let him know me and he took my virtue from me. Now I'm with child and he's dead. What am I going to do?"

"Oh dear," Amy finally understood what Brad had told her. Poor Belinda, she'd been deceived by a man who lied that he loved her and then he chased her away. She had given herself to an unworthy man and was now paying the price. "Belinda what happens now?"

"I'm going to kill myself because my aunt will never let me continue living in her house when she finds out. I'm starting to show and can't hide it anymore, Amy. What am I going to do?"

6

DEALING WITH THE PAST

Amy barely slept that night and lay on her small cot just thinking about how wonderful it would be to see Brad again. His beautiful hazel eyes that had the power to reduce her to a trembling mess, his thick dark hair, strong and yet gentle arms. It hadn't always been this way between them and she was worried that he probably didn't feel the same way for her after all these years.

London was filled with beautiful women who belonged to the high society and she was just a country bumpkin. His mother wanted a society wife for him and Amy was worried because Brad listened to his mother and obeyed her. What if he had found someone else, a woman who would meet with his mother's approval?

"Stop tormenting yourself," she whispered as she lay on the narrow cot. The only thing she could do was hold onto the promise he'd made her four years ago when he was leaving; that he would be back to marry her when she came of age. Brad had always been a man of his word and she had no reason to doubt that he would have changed even though there was still fear within.

Four years had passed during which she longed to write to him but didn't have his address. She was too timid to ask Mr. Pikes for it because her fear was that he would mention the fact to his wife and then Alice Pikes would descend on her with all the fury within her. But he should have at least written even if only once, just to let her know that he was thinking about her.

Early next morning, she was the first one up since Mrs. Pike had mentioned that Brad would be arriving on the morning train.

She set the dining room table and then went to the kitchen to start preparing breakfast. As she was stirring the oatmeal porridge in the large pot, she heard a carriage drive up to the front door. Brad was here and it felt like the sun had burst through the clouds and was shining down on her again. Excited and happy, she ran to the door, flung it open and got ready to rush into the arms of the man she loved. Oh what a glorious days, she thought, butterflies filling her stomach.

But as soon as she opened the door, Mrs. Pikes came from behind and shoved her aside. Amy went tumbling into the coat rack, bringing it crashing down. As she pulled herself up and straightened the coats and hats hanging on it, she heard voices coming from outside.

Taking a peek, she silently thanked Brad's mother for pushing her aside for what she saw tore at her heart. Brad stepped out of the carriage and then turned to help someone else down. It was a fragile looking woman and from where she was standing she could see that she was really beautiful. And pregnant! From the way Brad fussed over her once she was on the ground standing next to him, Amy was forced to admit that her fears had come true. She had lost Brad to one of the beautiful women of London.

So she ran back to the kitchen to hide her tears and lick her wounds in private. She didn't want to believe that Brad had betrayed her love, hope and trust like this and yet she'd seen it all with her own eyes. Where had all the sweet promises he'd made to her gone?

As she stirred the oatmeal on the stove and saw the flames dancing up towards the pot, she felt like her dreams had been licked up by the fiery inferno of life and reduced to nothing more than ashes.

"My Brad is here," Mrs. Pike burst into the kitchen. "And he's brought Isabelle with him. Isn't she beautiful?" And for the few minutes that she was running around the kitchen getting breakfast ready, the older woman was humming.

"Quick, Brad and his wife are hungry. They've been travelling for hours and as you know, Isabelle is with child. I'm going to be a grandmother and I'm so happy."

With each sentence that she spoke, Amy felt like Mrs. Pikes' words were driving a sharp arrow into her heart, twisting it around and then pulled it out with a force that caused her to bleed. The pain and anguish that she was feeling was so great that she wanted to double up and just crumble to the floor. But Amy had lived in this household for four years now and learned to hide her emotions from everyone.

It took great effort but she managed a smile, "That's really nice, Mrs. Pikes," she said.

"I'm happy that my son can no longer be ensnared by the wrong woman. And what's more, Isabelle is the granddaughter of a Count in Italy. She's nobility and that means that my grandchild may one day hold a title."

"Yes Ma'am," Amy responded dutifully, her smile in place while she was dying inside. She didn't know how much more verbal torture she could take but she wouldn't give this woman and her son the satisfaction of seeing her in pain.

Brad was talking to his father in the living room and Amy quickly put the served dishes on the dining table while praying that he wouldn't come and find her because she had no idea how she would react to him.

Once everything was arranged to Mrs. Pikes' satisfaction, Amy retired to the backyard and started sorting the laundry. She never joined the family for meals and would only eat once they were done.

Mrs. Pikes had made it clear that she was not a member of the family but an unpaid servant. After all, they were providing her with a bed to sleep in and food to eat, so she wasn't deserving of a salary.

Brad was glad to be home but he knew that things would be very tough given that he'd brought Isabelle with him.

He watched as his mother and sisters fussed over Isabelle, expressing their joy that he was married and she was expecting their first child. If only they knew!

The one person he longed to see was nowhere in sight though he'd caught a glimpse of her as she set the breakfast table. It surprised him that she was at their house this early but then thought that his mother had probably informed her that he was coming.

"How is Mrs. Chloe doing?" He asked May his sixteen year old sister.

"Oh, didn't you hear?" Naomi the fourteen year old piped up. "Mrs. Chloe died four years ago."

"Is that right?" He turned accusing eyes to his father who lowered his but not before Brad had seen the guilt in them. His mother pretended to be serving something onto Isabelle's plate and refused to look at him. "What happened to Amy then?"

The girls and their mother looked at each other and it was Naomi who answered him. "Amy came to live with us after her mother died."

"Oh?" He looked around the table. "Then where is she as we're taking breakfast? Shouldn't she be here with us? I thought I saw her setting the table."

His mother picked up the dish that contained smoked ham and held it out to Isabelle. "Would you like some?"

"Oh yes please, Mrs. Pikes," Isabelle said placing a hand on her stomach. "I didn't know that this baby would make me eat so much and I'm afraid that I'll soon resemble a well fed sow in a nightcap," she giggled.

"Nonsense," Mrs. Pikes waved her hand. "And please no more of that Mrs. Pikes nonsense. Please just call me Mama or Mother as Brad does."

"Thank you," Isabelle watched as Brad took the dish from his mother and placed a slice of ham on his plate as well as two baked potatoes. "This smells delicious, Mama."

"Thank you for saying that," Brad saw his mother's beaming smile. Much as he wanted to shout and demand that Amy to be allowed to join them at the table, he held his peace. There would be time to ask questions later when Isabelle was resting. After all they were still his parents and he had to show them respect in the presence of a guest in their home.

"I hope you'll enjoy your stay with us here, Isabelle," Mrs. Pikes said.

"You have a really nice home and I'm so glad Brad convinced me to come even though I tried to resist at first. Your son can be very convincing and that's why he's doing very well as a lawyer up in London, Mother." Isabelle had a soft voice with a faint accent.

Amy was skulking behind the kitchen door eavesdropping in on the conversation that was going on. She'd come in to get some washing powder and heard Brad asking about her. And she waited with bated breath to hear what explanation would be given as to her absence at the breakfast table. But Mrs. Pikes steered the conversation in a different direction. And Brad didn't insist on getting any answers nor did he demand that she be allowed to join the family at the breakfast table. He was truly gone from her and she tiptoed back outside, careful not to be found eavesdropping.

Amy was bent over the large pail, tears dropping into the soapy water when she became aware that she wasn't alone anymore. Not wanting Mrs. Pikes or her daughters to catch her weeping, she pretended to wash her face and then straightened up and turned, coming face to face with Brad.

Brad saw the deep pain in Amy's eyes before she lowered her eyelids and stepped behind the pail. "Good morning Mr. Bradford. Did you need anything?" She was being very polite and Brad wanted to rush towards her and take her into his arms and whisper that all would be well.

But his feet remained rooted to the place he was standing and he noted that she was really thin and pale. Her normally vibrant hair that he loved so much was lacklustre and had been tied at the back with an ugly ribbon. He liked that she'd allowed it to grow but it still looked like it was difficult to maintain. The huge pile of washing at her feet spoke volumes and his lips tightened. His father hadn't been exaggerating; his mother and sisters were working his Amy to death.

But before he could say anything, his mother appeared in the kitchen doorway.

"There you are, Brad. Your wife needs you," she told him. "I prepared your old bedroom and everything is ready." While there was a smile on her face, her eyes flashed angrily at Amy. "Go on, go and take care of my lovely daughter-in-law."

Brad wanted to resist and stay with Amy but it wasn't time yet. So he turned and kissed his mother's cheek. "Yes Mama, thank you for everything you've done to make Isabelle comfortable." And without a backward glance at Amy, he entered the house.

Amy knew she was in trouble when Mrs. Pikes bore down on her. "What nonsense were you telling my son?" She demanded.

"Nothing," she answered and for her efforts was rewarded with a backhand across her face. Tears sprang into her eyes and at that moment she happened to look up and saw Brad and Isabelle looking down into the courtyard, watching what was happening.

"Don't you dare answer me you insolent girl," and another slap followed the first.

To Amy nothing mattered anymore. The man who had promised to protect her just stood there watching his mother strike her and did nothing.

Something within her broke and she found herself on her knees wailing like she'd lost a beloved husband or child.

"Stop making all that racket or you'll feel the force of my wrath," Mrs. Pikes hissed at her. "Get back to work right now."

But Amy no longer had any strength to do anything other than weep. She expected more blows and got ready for them but nothing of the sort happened and after a brief moment, her tormenter left.

"Here, let me help you up," she heard Brad's voice and that filled her with rage. How dare he come anywhere near her after his betrayal and pretend to be concerned? "Amy, come, let me help you up."

"Get away from me," she hissed at him as she rose to her feet, ignoring his outstretched hand. "Don't ever come near me again, don't talk to me and don't even look my way," she wiped her tears on the sleeve of her dress. "Go back to your wife and pampered life and leave me alone. I don't want or need any trouble from you. Your pregnant wife is watching you from the upstairs window, just go away."

"Amy, things aren't what they seem to be."

"I don't want to hear anything more from you. Just go away," but he continued standing there as if he wanted to say something more. But Amy was done. She gave him an angry look and left the backyard, stepping into the lane behind the house. She quickened her steps as she heard Brad coming after her, ignoring him as he called for her to return.

From past experience Brad knew that it would take Amy time to calm down and he prayed that she would be alright. He watched as she walked away from him without a backward glance and disappeared around a corner.

With a sigh, he returned to the backyard and found Isabelle waiting for him.

"I was afraid of this happening," she laid a gentle hand on his arm. "Brad, the sacrifice you're making is too great. And Amy is paying for all this. Just see how badly your mother treats her. You shouldn't have allowed me to come with you."

"It's my choice and I would do it over and over again, Isabelle," he gave her a tender smile. "We came a long way and you look very tired, the best thing is for you to go upstairs and rest."

"How can I rest when I saw what happened? It's all my fault and I feel terrible about it. Do you think Amy will be alright?"

Brad sighed shaking his head. "What distresses me more is finding out that Amy has been suffering for four years. My parents and sisters have all been writing to me but no one ever told me that she'd lost her mother. They were very close and it must have been very painful for her. I made a promise to always be there to protect her but I've failed."

"I shouldn't have come," tears filled Isabelle's dark eyes. "What will happen to Amy? Do you think she'll be alright?"

"Whenever she got upset in the past, Amy would hide away for hours. Don't distress yourself. Amy will be back and then we'll put things right."

"I pray so because I don't want anything to happen to that sweet girl."

But Amy didn't return that day and not in the coming days either.

7
MEANS TO AN END

When Amy walked away from the Pikes' homestead she really had no intention of going very far. All she needed was time to clear her head as she thought about what to do next. It was clear that Brad and Isabelle would be staying for some time and she couldn't bear to see their happiness while her own was now nothing more than ashes. So she wanted to put as much distance between her and Brad as possible.

He'd broken her heart and betrayed her love but she was going to get through this. It wasn't the end of the world and more than anything, the young woman wished that her mother was still alive so she could go and cry in her arms. But she was all alone and life wasn't fair to her.

As she walked towards the beach where she'd had her last meeting with Brad four years ago, she ran into Belinda Taylor. The other girl was carrying a battered suitcase and looked very dejected.

"Belinda where are you going?"

"My aunt has kicked me out of her house and I have nowhere to go," she turned to Amy. "Can I come and live with you?"

Amy sighed, "Belinda, I wish I could help you but you know that I also don't have a home of my own. After Mama died four years ago, Mr. and Mrs. Pikes took me in and so I now live with them. I can't take you there because you know how Mrs. Pikes can be."

"I understand," Belinda gave her a tight smile. "You've been a good friend even when I wasn't kind to you in the past. And of all the people in this neighbourhood, you're the only one who still speaks to me and you are not ashamed to be seen with me."

The two young women walked in silence.

"Amy, you look really sad. I know Mrs. Pikes is a rather difficult person to put up with but don't you think it's time that you were going back now? I don't want her to scold you."

Amy gave a start especially when she noticed how far they had walked. Liverpool Railway Station was just a few yards ahead of them. The whole street was very busy with people coming and going and Amy wondered that she hadn't noticed in which direction she'd been walking.

"Why are we at the railway station, Belinda?"

"Because I'm leaving Liverpool for London. There's nothing left here for me."

"But what will you do once you get to London? It's a very dangerous and frightening place especially for a young woman alone."

Belinda shrugged, "I hear that there are many factories in London and I'll find work there so I can take care of myself and my baby since I have no one else in the world."

"But what about Chad's family? Don't they have a right to know that their son sired a child before he died?"

Belinda laughed softly, "They were the first people I went to when I found out that I was with child."

"What did they say?" Even as she asked the question Amy knew that her friend had received a hostile reaction to the news. And her next words confirmed Amy's suspicions.

"Amy, they said that I'm a woman of loose morals who was coming forward to claim that their angelic and holy son had sinned with me. Chad wasn't there to defend me and even if he had been, I doubt that he would have accepted that the child I'm carrying is his. After he had taken my virtue away, he chased me out of their house like a dog so whether dead or alive, that man is of no use to me. His parents wouldn't listen to me and so they too chased me away from their house."

"Oh Belinda, I'm so sorry that you had to go through all that."

"At least Philip believed me."

"Chad's older brother?"

Belinda nodded, "Yesterday he came by my Aunt's house and brought me twenty pounds. He told me that he was very sorry for the way his parents had treated me and wished there was something more that he could do."

"Why can't he come forward and help you out with the baby? What is twenty pounds?"

"Amy, I won't force anyone to help me when all this is my fault. And what's more, Philip is engaged to be married and the last thing I want is for any kind of scandal to ruin his plans for then he'll end up resenting me. My aunt overheard us talking and that's how she found out that I'm with child."

"But it's so obvious," Amy stared at her friend's protruding stomach. "How didn't your aunt notice this before?"

"I hid it well from her and you know that Aunt Monica isn't one who mixes with neighbours so she had no idea."

"Where in London are you headed?" An idea began forming in Amy's mind. "May I come with you?"

Belinda stopped walking and turned to face Amy. "Why?"

"It's a long story and I'll tell you as we go. May I please come with you? Two are better than one and when the baby comes, you'll need a lot of help. Besides that, at the time you get your baby, you won't be able to continue working for some time. So I'll work and take care of all of us."

"You would do that for me?"

Amy nodded, "It's more of also doing it for myself because there's nothing left for me here."

"But what about Brad? I heard that he had arrived and knowing how things were between the two of you before, shouldn't you be back at home with him?"

Amy blinked back the tears, "Belinda, Brad brought home a new wife, a pregnant one if I might add."

"Oh no!" Belinda was clearly horrified. "How could he do that to you?"

"His parents and especially his mother never felt that I was good enough for their son because I dropped out of school to take care of my mother when she was ill. Brad is now a successful lawyer in London and clearly wants nothing to do with a country bumpkin like me."

"Then come along," Belinda placed a light hand on Amy's arm. "Amy, we will get through this betrayal by the men we thought loved us. And as you say, two are better than one so yes, let's go to London together."

"But I don't have a single penny on me."

"The twenty pounds Philip gave me will suffice for our tickets to London and then some."

"Where exactly will we end up?"

"White Chapel. That's where we will find cheap lodgings and then it's a walking distance to many factories where we can find work."

The two girls beamed at each other. "Let's go in and get our tickets then." There was a spring in Belinda's step. And Amy felt that fate had decided for her to meet up with Belinda on this day that her life had fallen apart.

"I didn't even pack any clothes."

"You can share mine because I won't be wearing them for a while," Belinda smiled, placing a hand on her swollen stomach. "I was really scared about facing the future all alone with my baby but with you helping me out, I know that we'll be alright." And on impulse, Belinda hugged Amy. "Thank you."

"Don't thank me yet," Amy felt happier than she'd been in quite a while. "You don't know what the future holds."

"No, I don't but it's now less frightening because I won't be facing it alone. Now, let's go and get our tickets, and then we can find our train and board it."

And arm in arm, the two young women walked to the ticket office smiling like they didn't have a care in the world. But both were somewhat worried about what lay ahead of them. Still, they were sure that together they could meet and overcome any obstacles and challenges that life threw at them.

Later that afternoon Brad called his sisters to the backyard. "I'm really worried about Amy. She went out a while ago but hasn't returned. Do you know where she could be?"

May turned her nose up, "She must be with that Belinda girl, a worthless one like herself."

"I'll slap you so hard that your ears will be ringing for a whole year," he growled at her.

"Ma," May called out, tears in her eyes and her mother came running. "Ma, Brad wants to slap me."

"Why?"

"Because I told him that Amy had gone to be with Belinda the pregnant girl."

Brad looked at his mother and saw her lip curling in scorn. "I always knew that girl to be trouble and quite worthless. She's been talking with Belinda who got pregnant out of wedlock by one of the sailors at the docks and then had the effrontery to blame it on poor Chadwick. It isn't possible that Chad could have fathered her child because he died days ago. Those two girls have been going around with all kinds of men and it's just a matter of time before Amy is like Belinda, carrying an illegitimate child and bringing shame on us. Why did I ever agree with your father to keep her in my house? She might have taught my daughters her bad behaviour and if she's chosen to go and stay with her worthless friend then it's good riddance for me."

"You still haven't told me where I can find Amy," Brad said stubbornly. "And you can save your insults Mother. Amy is a good girl and her mother raised her right so I don't think she has done any of those things you're accusing her of."

"That girl has blinded you and you're not seeing anything else, Brad. Your wife is upstairs sleeping and here you are asking about a woman who doesn't deserve any kind of respect."

"Is that why you've been tormenting her while she was living under this roof?"

"She's lazy and how else is she supposed to earn her keep? I can't feed and clothe a woman who refuses to go out there and find work. Since she decided that she doesn't want to work, I made her serve me in this house."

Brad gave his mother a long hard look before turning away and walking towards the backyard gate.

"And where do you think you're going?"

"I'm going to find Amy and bring her back home. If you don't want her here then I'll take her up to London with me."

"You'll do no such thing, Bradford. Come back right now."

But he ignored her, feeling pain in his heart at what had happened to Amy. Why hadn't he returned years ago and taken her away like he'd promised? He had left her alone and couldn't imagine the anguish she'd felt when her mother died and he didn't attend the burial. But in his defence he hadn't known that Mrs. Chloe had died. His family had kept the secret well hidden and Amy had suffered for it.

It was time to find her and make things right or he would never have peace again.

8

INTO WICKED CLUTCHES

It soon became apparent to the two young women that the London of their dreams was much different from actual reality. On their journey, they had talked about the amazing experience that awaited them upon their arrival. London was the city where the Queen lived, the centre of England's very existence. They would work hard and rise above their poverty to become women of substance.

The first thing they did when they got to Euston Railway Station was to embark on their search for lodgings. An old man with an equally old taxi buggy conveyed them to White Chapel while upsetting them with gruesome stories of the murders of two young women which had just recently been reported. He thought he was entertaining them but they were so frightened and clasped their fingers together, wishing he would just stay silent.

"You make sure you take care now," he said, spitting some black stuff from his mouth onto the sidewalk. A passerby jumped aside just in time to avoid the spittle being splattered all over his shoes and though he gave the taxi driver an ugly look, the old man didn't seem to notice it. "No staying out at night and wandering these streets. Them is not safe," he said, and tipped his dirty hat at them before joining the traffic back to Euston Station.

"I've never seen a noisier or dirtier street," Amy shuddered. They were standing at the junction of Old Castle and Gun. She'd always thought Sheffield was an untidy little suburb but seeing this side of London made her change her mind.

"We just have to make do with what has been handed to us," Belinda said. "I can't believe that I'm finally in London. It's such a big city and I can't wait to explore it."

Amy looked at her in surprise.

"Why are you staring at me like that?" Belinda asked her.

"Because you're one in a million, Belinda. Here I was ready to start complaining about this city but all you see is the goodness in it. You humble me and I promise that I won't complain again."

"The one thing that I want to see most is the London Bridge and cross the River Thames from one side to the other. Someone told me that it's really beautiful."

Amy laughed, a happy sound that made people turn to look at the beautiful red haired young woman who looked like she didn't have a single care in the world.

"I know just what you mean," she told Belinda, linking her hand in hers. "My own desire is to see Queen Victoria's palace and maybe catch a glimpse of her. She's one of the luckiest women in the world and she must be so happy because she has everything a woman can ever want."

"Dearest Amy, you're so simple and naïve as to believe that wealth and other worldly goods bring joy and happiness in a person's life. The Queen has been in mourning for years after her husband's death and it is rumoured that she is very sad and continues to wear her garments of widowhood several years after her husband died. She hardly ever leaves her home to be seen in public. Amy, you and I are happier than she is even though our circumstances are so dire right now. We have the freedom of living our lives without being subjected to numerous scandals and having people always wanting to know what is going on."

"And again Belinda I'll say that you've set me straight. I guess I was just feeling a little down because my Brad chose a wealthy woman over me," she shook her head. Though she was still very sad about Brad's betrayal, being hundreds of miles away from him helped. "I'll try to find happiness in the everyday little things."

"I also learned this the hard way and so I'm determined to take it one day at a time. We can't speak for tomorrow but as we have been given grace to see today, let's make the most of it," she looked around her. "Where do we even start?"

"We could walk down these alleys and streets and see if we can first find jobs." Amy had never seen so many people all crowded in the same place. She kept being shoved from side to side but never loosened her grip on the carpetbag she was carrying. It contained all their meagre possessions and losing it would be a huge setback.

"But we have to find a place to bed for the night. You heard that old man and what he said, that the streets aren't safe at night. Whitechapel may look harmless by day but I'm sure that it teems with evil at night."

It was early afternoon and they walked for nearly two hours without any success. Everywhere they saw a vacancy sign and asked they were turned away because the owners of the establishment said they looked suspicious.

"We have no vacancy for women of the night," one woman was bold as to say to their faces.

"I can't take much more of this," Belinda said tears spilling from her eyes.

"I know that you're tired but we can't give up yet. Let's do this," Amy looked around for somewhere that Belinda could sit. Her feet were swollen and she looked really exhausted. It was a narrow street and there was no park nearby but just some sidewalk cafes. "Why don't you sit in that small café and let me find somewhere then I'll come and get you."

Belinda shook her head, "No with all the crowding in this place, you'll never find me again. Let's not be separated because I'm beginning to be afraid. We'll continue searching," she said with new resolve, linking her arm in Amy's. "You're just as tired and please forgive me for being so childish. Let's both go to another street and search again. We'll find something."

Once again arm in arm, they made their way down one or two crowded streets. Everywhere they looked they saw signs for lodgings that were available but the rent being asked was too high. Four pence per day was more than they could afford since they didn't as yet have jobs.

Finally dejected and tired they came upon an old building. It was four stories high and hard dark windows, reminding Amy of one of the factory warehouses back in Liverpool. They noticed a queue of about thirty young women outside the main door and on impulse decided to join it. The sign above the large door said *South End Matches Factory.* It was disheartening to see some women being turned away and one who stubbornly refused to move was hauled out of there like a sack of potatoes by two burly men and practically tossed into a filthy puddle of water. Amy wondered what the criteria for admission into this place was and prayed that she and Belinda would meet the cut. A few more women were turned away but soon it was their turn.

When they got to the front of the queue, Amy came face to face with a very stern looking woman who looked to be in her fifties. She was wearing a dark blue tunic over which was an apron and from the way she conducted herself, Amy deduced that she was a senior supervisor.

"Name," the woman barked.

"Amelia Baxter."

"Age?"

"Twenty one years old, Ma'am," Amy lied.

"Are you married?"

"No Ma'am."

"Do you have any children?"

"No Ma'am."

"Get in," and she was practically shoved into the warehouse by one of the guards. She prayed that Belinda would also be let in and when she saw her friend a few minutes later, smiled with happiness.

They followed other girls who had also made the cut and soon found themselves in a large room. There were tables lined up along all four walls and in the middle of the room. As they stood there looking lost, another middle aged woman walked towards them.

"Welcome to South End Matches Factory Women's Hostel," she smiled at the group of young women standing before her. She was dressed the same as the woman who had admitted them into the building. "My name is Helen Wright and I'm the women's matron. This means that I'm responsible for all your welfares. Why don't you follow me?"

She turned and the women followed her. Amy looked around and wondered if things would go well for them. The walls were white washed as were the tables and benches. The floor was old and broken up in places giving the place an untidy look even though it was clean.

"This isn't the factory," Helen said, "But the women's hostel. The factory is on the other side of this building and tomorrow all of you will be taken to your respective places of work. You'll stick to the places that have been set up for you and no snooping or sneaking out. Two meals are served each day and that is breakfast and dinner. The expense will be deducted from your wages every Friday. It's nearly dinner time and once you're done eating, I'll show you to your quarters."

Amy could see the relief and confusion on her peers' faces and the same emotions were mirrored on her own but no one dared ask how much they would be paid and what would be deducted from it. The place was dry and there was the promise of bed and food as well as jobs which was more than they could say for the others.

After dinner, which consisted of a pulpy mash that tasted like potatoes and pumpkins as well as a thin bean soup, Helen came and rounded up the new girls. There were about thirty of them, all young and pretty and between the ages of sixteen and twenty four. She took them up one flight of stairs and pushed open a large wooden door to reveal a long room, with darkened windows, which had about twenty well made beds.

"Given that you're all new, you'll have the probationary dormitory because we first have to find out if you'll stay or if we have to send you away," Helen smiled to soften her words. "In this dormitory two people have to share a bed. Once you pass your probationary period which is two weeks, you'll then be moved to the main dormitory upstairs where you'll each have a bed to yourselves. Girls, I hope you understand how lucky and blessed you are to have been allowed in here. The factory owner is a Christian and so every morning at four thirty a.m. you'll be woken up for prayers until five. After which you'll be allowed to prepare for the day. The breakfast gong sounds at exactly five thirty. If you're late you'll miss breakfast and there's no other meal served in between until you return in the evening for dinner. Lights are switched off at nine P.M. and I expect everyone to obey the rules here. Laziness, untidiness and rudeness won't be tolerated and if found, your employment will be immediately terminated and then you'll be sent packing. Also if you sneak out of here, don't bother coming back because you won't be readmitted."

Belinda raised her hand.

"Yes young lady?"

"Ma'am, is provision made for natural needs in the night?"

Helen pointed at two covered metal pails in the corner of the dormitory. "Use them and empty them in the morning when you go to the bathrooms. Once it's nine P.M.. and the lights are off, the doors are locked and won't be opened until four. It's for your own safety so see to it that no one tries to sneak out."

Amy was determined that she and Belinda wouldn't be kicked out of their new home. It didn't look so bad and they could have ended up in a worse place. As they had been walking through the streets and alleys of Whitechapel, they'd seen many ugly and dilapidated doss- houses and seeing the residents seated on the shaky balconies the one thing Amy had noted was the hopelessness and despair etched on their faces.

"We are really lucky," Belinda whispered as they got under the blanket once the lights had been switched off. "I felt very sorry for those women who were turned away and was praying that we would be accepted."

"It looks like a nice place," Amy agreed. "At least we'll be able to make some money. Let's put aside a little money every week until we have enough to find a small shop to lease so we can start our own bakery."

"Amy you're such a dreamer," Belinda chuckled. "Do you know how expensive it is to start one's own bakery?"

"Brad once told me that his father started with nothing but an old second hand stove and a determination to succeed. And see how far Mr. Pikes has come. I believe that we can also do the same."

"What will you do if you ever come across Brad again? Remember that he lives here in London and it's inevitable that your paths will one day cross."

Amy didn't want to think about that. "I doubt that Brad will find his way down to these slums, Belinda. He's a successful lawyer and with a high society wife so they'll stick to the better places of London. So I highly doubt that our paths will ever cross."

"You just never know with this life," Belinda murmured sleepily. "I'm just glad that we have a place to sleep for tonight, and a good one at that. Goodnight Amy."

"Goodnight Belinda." And silence reigned in the dormitory. But even as Amy started drifting off to sleep one thing stood out; they still had no idea how much money they would be paid at the end of every week.

Early the next morning after breakfast that consisted of watery oatmeal porridge and a thin slice of bread, the thirty new girls were separated into five different groups of six each and sent off in different directions.

Amy and her five new acquaintances were led through a door that she hadn't noticed earlier to a room that made her eyes widen. They were met at the door by a slender woman who had a wide smile but Amy noticed that her eyes were cold. This looked like a luxury parlour like those she'd seen back in Liverpool that catered to rich women who wanted to be pampered and have their hair styled.

"Why are we here?" She whispered to one of the other girls who merely shrugged.

"Ladies, please take your seats," the slender lady said. "My name is Pearl and I'll be taking care of you for the next few days." They were pointed to large cushioned chairs and immediately they sat down, six women appeared as if by magic and began pampering them. Their feet were scrubbed, nails were trimmed and shaped, their hair shampooed and then brushed until it shone. Amy's scalp was tingling but she daren't complain for fear of being thrown out. It also felt good having her unruly hair secured with a number of pins and side combs.

Once their grooming was over, they were taken to a second room where they were given tight fitting gowns. Amy felt like a ragdoll as she was stuffed into a green dress that was too tight and showed off her cleavage in a way that brought the colour to her face. These were the kind of clothes that her mother would never have allowed her to wear and she would have received a thorough flaying for even thinking about them.

Something didn't quite feel right to her and she looked around to see if any of the others were as uncomfortable as she was. One or two looked scared but the others were excited at the grooming and new dresses they were given. Finally they were given new sandals and taken to another room where another middle aged woman was waiting for them.

"You're the chosen ones," she told them. "You have been selected to perform special duties and each morning you'll be taken to your places of work and brought back in the evening. Just know that your wages are one and a half times more than your peers and if you perform well then you'll get bonuses. What's more when you return this evening, you'll each be taken to a private room so you don't have to stay with the rest of the women."

The other five new girls clapped enthusiastically but Amy did so half-heartedly. Something very strange was going on here and she didn't like it one bit.

"Now, follow me," the woman said. She hadn't even introduced herself. They were taken down a dimly lit narrow corridor at the end of which they emerged into a small lane at the back of the building. There were six carriages waiting and the six of them were each bundled into their own. No two girls shared a carriage and Amy was now really uncomfortable.

The moment Amy was seated, the carriage shot forward and she decided that she wanted to go back to the factory.

"Take me back," she banged on the wall of the carriage. If the driver heard her he showed no signs of it. "Where are you taking me?" She was shouting but the carriage only went faster. She tried to open one of the windows but it was stuck fast as was the door and she realized that she was practically a prisoner in this vehicle.

After pounding on the wall for a while she realized that she was only exhausting herself. So she sat back quite tired and frightened. This was no ordinary factory job that she was being taken to and began to have her own frightful suspicions.

The carriage drove over a cobbled path and when she looked out, saw that they were in the courtyard of an imposing manor.

The carriage stopped and the door was opened from the outside.

"Get down," a harsh voice barked the order from outside the carriage. She saw the driver turn to look at her but his face was a mask of total indifference and she knew that she would get no help from him. He had probably been paid a hefty sum to bring her to this place. She shrank into the farthest corner of the carriage heart pounding. "Young lady, I said get down at once."

"No."

"Miss, if I have to bring you out then you'll be very sorry."

But Amy was unable to move. She had no idea where she was or what would happen to her and her whole body stiffened. The carriage driver muttered something and entered the carriage.

"Get down now, Miss," he told her in a rough voice. "I need to return and go on another errand and if you delay me then I'll miss out on a commission."

Amy shook her head. Fear is what kept her stuck on the seat. The man's beefy hand shot out and he grabbed her by the neck.

"You're one of those who wants to cause me trouble, right?" He handled her roughly and pushed her out of the carriage. She landed on her knees and before she could even rise to her feet, a whip lash landed hard on her back and she cried out.

"If you behave like a lady then you'll be treated like one. But if you want to behave like a petulant child then be prepared for the consequences. Now up on your feet," the harsh voice commanded and she scrambled to her feet, feeling the sting of the lash.

She heard the carriage driver getting back onto his vehicle and she wished she could beg him to get her out of there. But he drove off and she was left standing with her head bowed before a tall and heavyset man.

A large hand grabbed her chin roughly and raised her head, forcing her to look into the face of her assailant.

"I like those who resist like you for then it gives me the pleasure of breaking you down," he said and she looked into very cold green eyes. The man looked slightly deranged and Amy feared the worst. She wasn't getting out of this without being harmed and she began to pray for death. Something about the man looked familiar but she was sure that she'd never seen him in her life before.

"And you'll address me as 'Master,'" he said.

"Yes Master," she mumbled because the man's hand was squeezing her jaw and she was in pain. It was still early morning and very cold and she longed for the warmth of the carriage but it was long gone.

"I like stubborn ones like you," the man laughed, a sound that drove fear into Amy's heart. "I'll break you and reduce you to nothing more than my slave. Before this day is over, you'll be begging me on your knees."

He turned and with a flick of his wrist motioned to someone. A middle aged man approached and when Amy looked into his eyes, she saw something akin to pity. But he quickly averted his eyes as he handed his master a rope.

The tall man bound her wrists tightly and she cried out as the coarse rope cut into her delicate skin.

"On your knees at once," Amy complied with the order and the tall man dragged her along into the manor as one would an animal. By the time they had walked over the cobbled stones and into the hallway, Amy's knees were scraped and bleeding and tears were pouring down her face.

But even as she feared for her own life and whatever would happen to her, she thought about Belinda and prayed that her friend wouldn't be subjected to such inhumane treatment.

Her 'master' dragged her through the hallway and up the stairs, using the whip when he felt that she was slowing down. Under better circumstances, she would have appreciated the fine artwork that lined the well lit hallway, the beautiful furniture she caught a glimpse of as he dragged her along the marbled floor. But all she could think about was what she'd ever done to deserve such terrible things happening to her.

She knew that her virtue was in danger and for a brief moment anger stirred up within her breast. This was all Brad's fault. Had he not betrayed her trust and love, she would never have thought about leaving the safety of Liverpool. Even living in Mrs. Pikes' household and being subjected to her cruel treatment was better than what was bound to happen to her in the next few minutes.

The man finally opened the door to a large room and Amy got some relief as her knees rode over a thick soft carpet. The curtains were open and the room was brightly lit allowing her to see the huge canopy bed in the centre. There was also a large couch standing along one of the walls and a dresser on the opposite side. Even though the whole room was done in rich colours of gold, brown and cream to Amy this was a prison and she couldn't imagine the horrors that awaited her here.

"Beg me for your honour and your life," the man said. "Come on, beg me," he shouted, bringing down the whip over her back. "Look at your lord and master when he's speaking to you," and Amy raised tear filled eyes to him. There was a glint in his eyes that made her realize that she was dealing with a completely deranged man who took pleasure in hurting others.

She was going to be badly hurt and probably killed and felt like she had nothing to lose. But she wasn't going to give the man the satisfaction of hearing her begging for her life.

So she bowed her head and refused to talk. She was weary and felt like her spirit was completely broken. Nothing in life had prepared her for such ill treatment and all she could think about at that moment was her mother.

"Mama," she wept, "Why did you have to die and leave me alone in this cruel world," she murmured.

Though they had lived a simple life and not had material wealth, Amy had been sure of her mother's love. Even when things were difficult when her mother had fallen ill, they had prayed together and kept talking about better days ahead.

But her mother was gone forever and she'd been left all alone to suffer and now felt completely drained. So deep was her despair and anguish that she didn't feel the lashes that landed on her back in quick succession, mercilessly tearing through her flesh and causing her to bleed. It was like her captor had been taken over by a frenzy of insanity and when he realized that she wasn't even crying out in pain, grabbed her dress and ripped it, exposing both of her shoulders.

Amy didn't hear the loud gasp or see the look of horror that crossed the man's face, nor see him stumbling backwards until he fell onto the couch and sat there staring at her with shock.

With a soft sigh, she pitched forward as darkness took over.

"I'll never forgive you for this, Mother," Brad looked down at his mother who was seated on the couch. She had covered her face with her hands and was weeping. "You were the one who always told me that we should be kind to widows, orphans and the needy and I strove to emulate your Christian virtue of kindness, gentleness and generosity. Yet when Amy came to live in this house all you did was make her life a living hell. Where was your Christianity when day by day for four years you made that young girl suffer?"

"I'm sorry," Mrs. Pikes sobbed.

"Why are you now sorry, Mother? Papa told me that at the time of her death Mrs. Chloe gave you five hundred pounds and also instructions to find Amy's real parents. But instead you turned her into your slave and you now sit here saying that you're sorry. Right before my own eyes, I saw you strike an innocent woman who had done you no wrong." He turned his gaze to his sisters. "Did the two of you not feel compassion for the girl who had always been part of this family? Was she not someone's daughter? Instead you tormented her and made her go through so much pain. Now Amy has gone somewhere and only God knows where she could be and what is happening to her." He turned to his father. "Papa, how could you let something so evil take place under your roof without saying anything?"

"Son, please forgive us," Peter said. "I take full responsibility for everything that happened and will do anything to find Amy and bring her back home."

"Papa, I love and respect you but right now please don't try to appease me. You had the chance to make things right for four years yet you wouldn't do anything about it. What's more, you never once told me that Mrs. Chloe had passed away. I was very busy working hard in London as an apprentice so I could make you proud and earn a good living. From when I was young, you knew what my intentions towards Amy were. I love her and had promised to take care of her and protect her too. Had you told me that Mrs. Chloe died, I would have come and taken her away and so prevented all this from happening."

He sat down and bowed his head, feeling quite frustrated. Days had gone by and still there was no sign of Amy. He'd even gone as far as Belinda's house and been met by a very harsh looking woman who told him that she hadn't set eyes on Amy.

"What has happened to my sister?" Isabelle was weeping and the three women looked at her in surprise.

"Sister?" Alice squealed.

Isabelle pulled off the dark wig from her head and red curls tumbled out. She also lowered the neckline of her gown on the left side to reveal a large dark mark.

"For centuries this has been referred to as the Cavanaugh Streak. Every child born to a Cavanaugh male whether boy or girl inherits two or three distinct marks that show they carry the family blood. This birthmark, bright red curly hair and green eyes are the ultimate sign of one being a Cavanaugh. But my mother is Italian and I inherited her dark eyes. Still, I have the hair and birthmark of my paternal family. Others are born with different colour hair but have green eyes and the mark. This particular birthmark is on all of us."

No one said a word.

"Brad and my husband…"

"What do you mean?" Alice quickly looked up.

Isabelle gave her a tight smile. "Brad and I aren't married. We chose this disguise because I wanted to be sure that Amelia was really of my blood. That's why I had to don a wig so no one could see the resemblance before I was ready. I needed to confirm that Amy is really related to me. It has been my desire to find all those who are related to me by blood and my grandparents on Papa's side have supported this endeavour."

Brad took Isabelle's hand. "We'll work together and find Amy," his voice was soft. "No matter where she is, I'll move heaven and earth until I find her. And when I do, I will take her away from people who have made her life so miserable. Never again will I let any of you near Amy and once I leave this house, you'll never see me again."

"Brad no," his mother held out her hand which he ignored.

Rising to his feet, he helped Isabelle up. "We're going to pack and leave right away. I can't stand to spend a single moment in this house."

"Son," Peter called out. "Please temper your justice with mercy. We've wronged you and deserve your ire. But we're still your parents and family and beg you to forgive us."

"Father, you didn't wrong me at all. Think about Amy and how she loved and respected you like a father. A father is supposed to protect his offspring and not let them be cruelly treated."

"I failed as a father but I'm ready to do anything to find Amy and bring her back home. What can I do to make things right?"

Brad gave his father a long look and then turned and walked out of the room without saying another word.

9

VALLEY OF SHADOWS

When Amy opened her eyes, she found herself lying on her side on a soft mattress. Her whole body ached and she moaned, moving restlessly on the bed. A gentle hand was placed on her brow.

"Hush child," a soft voice said and Amy heard the tremor in the person's voice, like that of one who was crying. Her eyes felt heavy and once again she slipped into merciful oblivion.

The next time she woke up she was able to fully open her eyes and noticed that she was in a large and airy room. It had pretty white and yellow curtains adorning the large window that spanned the whole length of one side of the wall. Never had she seen such a pretty room and suddenly she felt like she couldn't breathe.

She was lying in a bed and had no clothes on save something heavy on her back. So she panicked and started screaming, thrashing wildly when she remembered what had happened to her.

"Let me die," she sobbed in anguish as soft hands held her firmly on her side, preventing her from falling on her back. "Please just let me die."

She was sure that the evil man had violently robbed her of her virtue, the one thing she had guarded with her whole heart and kept for Brad. Now she was all broken up and didn't want to live any more. She felt like whatever had happened to Belinda would be her fate and she would end up with a baby she never wanted from an act of violence. "Just leave me to die."

"Child, you're breaking my heart," the woman's voice broke. "Please calm down and let me take care of you."

Amy closed her eyes and wept brokenly. Why hadn't she died as an infant in her mother's womb? For then she would have been spared all the pain and anguish that had happened in the past four years.

Life was not worth living because her love had been betrayed and she'd ended up in the hands of a monster who had done terrible things to her while she lay unconscious.

Amy felt the woman moving away from the bed even as the door opened.

"I'm really worried about her," she heard the woman speaking to someone.

"Have the wounds on her back festered? Are you taking the bandages off every few hours and cleaning the wounds?"

"Yes doctor, we've done all that you instructed us to do and her back is healing nicely."

"What then is the problem?"

"Her spirit is broken," the woman sniffed. "My poor grandchild has suffered and what's worse at the hands of her own father."

"Mrs. Cavanaugh, I'm very sorry for all the tragedies that have befallen you in the past few days."

"Dr. Jordan, is there anything you can do to help this poor child? To think that she was out there in the world all alone and of all the places that she could have landed in, her father's house and hands. I knew my youngest son was bad but finding out that he'd turned into a monster is something I can't bear to think about."

"At least he did the right thing before he took his own life."

"Saving grace," the woman's voice seemed to fade away as Amy slipped into deep sleep.

It was hours later when she once again regained consciousness. She turned to lie on her back and cried out in pain. No one came to the bed and she realized that she was alone in the room. Groaning audibly, she rolled onto her stomach and raised herself until she was kneeling on the bed then slowly stepped down and her feet landed on a soft carpet. There was a silky dressing gown on the chair by the bed and she reached for it, feeling the shame of being naked even though she was alone in room. Her knees were red and she felt tears as she recalled being dragged across the cobblestones, down a hallway and up the stairs like an animal being taken to the slaughterhouse. Amy had never believed that human beings were capable of such wickedness.

Her back felt really sore. At least her hands and feet weren't bound and once she was on her feet, she swayed a little. She staggered to the window and stood looking out into the courtyard below. It was clearly the back of the house for she could see stables and beyond that a large green field. Spring was in the air and that signified the newness of life. But all she felt was dead and vast emptiness inside.

She recalled the conversation she'd overheard as she was drifting into sleep. The woman with the soft voice had said she was her grandchild. Where was this and how had she gotten here from that den of torture?

The door opened and she quickly turned to find a beautiful and elegant woman standing there. She reminded Amy of Isabelle, Brad's wife and she was confused.

"Child, I'm happy to see that you're awake and have returned to us."

"Who are you and where am I?" Amy asked cautiously, pulling the gown even closer to her body as if to hide from something. This might be another trick to lure her into more trouble.

"Please sit down for you're still very weak. You lost a lot of blood and at one point, I despaired of your life," tears shimmered in the older woman's eyes.

Amy was glad that the woman made no move to come any closer or touch her. So she walked slowly back to the bed and sat down, watching the other woman keenly. She had no idea why she'd been brought into this household and she had to be careful not to be deceived with smooth words and false hope again.

"Who are you?" Amy repeated the question.

"My name is Hortensia Cavanaugh and I'm your grandmother."

Amy stared at her for a full minute without saying a word. "I don't have a grandmother so you're lying," while her voice wasn't loud her tone was hard. She was done with deceitful people and as soon as she felt stronger, she would find a way out of this house.

"Please tell me your name," the woman ignored her outburst.

"Amelia Jane Baxter. And my mother told me that we have no living relatives so lady, I don't know who you are or why you've brought me here but I want to leave."

"Amelia listen to me," the smile was gone. "You're a very intelligent young woman and a fair one I guess.

So before you judge or dismiss me, please just give me the chance to explain and answer your questions."

"Go on but do it fast because I need to leave."

"My husband and I bore six children; four girls at first and then we stopped for some years. When we had despaired of having any sons, the Lord blessed us with two. Hugh is our eldest and Edgar was born three years after him." Amy saw the sorrow on the woman's face but hardened her heart. She still needed an explanation as to why she was here.

"From when my sons were babies, my husband and I overindulged them. We gave them whatever they asked for and also we kept excusing their behaviour and saying they were still small. As they grew older and we realized the kind of boys they were becoming, we decided to change the way we were treating them. Our sons were selfish and self-centred, even being prejudiced against their own sisters. So we sent them to boarding school with the hope that they would get discipline from the schoolmasters there and be taught to be better people. Hugh changed and soon sobered up and settled down. When he finished school, he came to work with his father. But Edgar," Mrs. Cavanaugh wiped her eyes. "My last son was really wild. He fell into the wrong crowd at school and was nearly expelled more than once. His father gave him an ultimatum; to either change and be a better person or leave our home and be cut off for good. Edgar chose the latter option."

10

WINTER IS GONE

A my's stomach growled like an angry bear and her face turned red. She couldn't recall the last time she'd had any kind of food nor could she tell what day it was and how long she'd been in this house.

"Oh my dear," Hortensia shot to her feet. "I'm mortified that I've not thought about feeding you." She picked up the small bell on the bedside table and rang it, a tinkling musical sound that reminded Amy of a small toy that Brad had brought her from London nearly six years ago. He called it a music box and she'd spent hours just gazing at it and listening to the sweet sound it produced. But on the day that she'd gone to live with the Pikes, Naomi saw it and grabbed it, dropping it and it had splintered into little pieces. Amy had wept for it was the only connection she had with Brad and had received a few slaps from Mrs. Pikes when Amy had demanded that Naomi should restore it to its original shape.

"You look really sad," Mrs. Cavanaugh said about the look on Amy's face. "As if you suddenly remembered something that you had lost."

Amy raised her shoulders then dropped them again. Her stomach growled a second time and she tried to muffle the sound by holding a pillow close to her body.

"You were in and out of consciousness for a week and all we were able to feed you was a little soup and milk. You must be really hungry."

So she'd been unconscious for seven days. Seven days of her life that she would never get back! Amy wanted to scream but then felt the walls around her heart cracking when she looked into her grandmother's face.

"Are you really my grandmother?" She found herself asking. Her emotions were quite raw and she longed to feel her mother's warm arms around her.

Hortensia nodded. "Amelia?"

"Amy," she found herself saying. "You can call me Amy if you want to."

"Thank you," Mrs. Cavanaugh gave her a small smile. "Let the maid bring you something to eat and then I'll continue with the story."

After a few minutes, a maid brought her some chicken soup which smelled so wonderful and Amy salivated for the meal.

"The doctor advised that because you haven't eaten anything for a while, we should start you off on soft meals like soup."

Mrs. Cavanaugh picked up the bowl of hot broth and sat beside Amy. "Are you able to feed yourself?" she asked softly, blowing over the hot soup. Tears filled Amy's eyes as she remembered that her mother used to do the same thing for her.

"Please don't cry," Mrs. Cavanaugh used one hand to wipe the tears from Amy's face. "Eat first and then we'll talk some more."

Amy tried to lift the silver spoon but found that it was too heavy and her hand was weak, so it clattered back onto the tray. "I'm sorry."

"Here, please let me help," Mrs. Cavanaugh placed the bowl back on the bedside table then picked up a slice of fresh bread, tore it into pieces and dipped them into the broth. She then fed Amy, being careful to blow over each spoonful.

When Amy was replete, she turned her head away. "No more."

"Thank you for letting me come close to you," Mrs. Cavanaugh placed the near empty bowl back on the tray then turned to Amy. "Would you like to lie down now?"

Amy shook her head. She knew that the moment her head touched the pillow, she would be out like light and yet she needed to hear the story to the end. At least the food she'd just eaten had taken care of one of the problems. "Please go on with your story."

"My last born child and son Edgar was the Black Sheep of the family. After he chose to go his own way, I tried to reach out to him and begged him to come back home. But he never came home unless his father and I were away. And most times that he showed up, it was just to ask Hugh for money to waste with his friends," she fell silent. "Hugh married a young Italian woman who he met at his sister's wedding in Paris nearly twenty years ago. He brought Rosalie back home with him and she gave him only one child, a daughter," a smile of fondness crossed the woman's face. "Isabelle is the love of her father but…"

"Isabelle?" Amy whispered. What were the odds of finding out that Mrs. Cavanaugh's granddaughter was half Italian and named Isabelle like the woman who had stolen her beloved Brad away from her?

"Amy are you alright?" Mrs. Cavanaugh's anxious voice broke through her thoughts. She wanted to tell her newly found grandmother everything but first needed to know more.

"I just feel tired," Amy said which was partly true.

"Why don't you lie down for a little bit and I'll sit here with you?"

"I don't want to fall asleep again," Amy really tried to stay awake because she was afraid that if she fell asleep, she might wake up to find out that she was still in the clutches of that monster and that this sense of peace and wellbeing was just a dream.

"Even if you fall asleep I won't leave your side and will continue with the story when you wake up. I'd like for you to understand how you ended up in our home."

"Alright then," Amy allowed herself to be tucked into bed. This woman reminded her so much of her mother and she longed to reach out and hug her. "Go on," she said instead.

"Where was I?"

"You were telling me about Isabelle."

"Oh yes," Mrs. Cavanaugh smiled. "She's such a sweet girl and my first grandchild from my sons. Of course, my four daughters have given me grandchildren, ten between them. But those belong to their husbands' families. When Isabelle was born, Rosa nearly lost her life. Once she had recovered, Hugh took them back to Italy for the weather here was terrible. They ended up living there for nearly fifteen years. But they would visit us every summer. Hugh continued to work here in London and so was away from his family for over six months each year. In that time, he sired three more children with different women, two boys and one girl. Rosa couldn't have any more children after the difficult labour that nearly took her life. When Hugh told me this, I looked for my grandchildren and brought them back to the fold. You'll meet them all when you're back on your feet. They're really sweet children." Mrs. Cavanaugh twisted her lips. "My son's indiscretions nearly wrecked his marriage but Rosa is so forgiving and always took him back. I used to say that my husband bore the mark of a curse but it has turned out to be a great blessing to me and my family."

"I don't understand."

Mrs. Cavanaugh's response was to reach over and lower the blanket from Amy's shoulders. She then slid the night gown from off her left shoulder. "That right there," she pointed at the ugly mark that Amy hated so much. "That's the Cavanaugh Streak as people have referred to it for generations. Every child whether a boy or girl who is born to a son of this family bears that mark. My daughters all have it but their children don't. However, all Hugh's children have it."

"So I'm Hugh's daughter?" Amy thought she was dreaming.

Mrs. Cavanaugh shook her head. "You're Edgar's daughter."

"The Black Sheep? How then did I get here?"

"Seven days ago, one of Edgar's male servants came to our house. He was quite agitated and could barely speak. He'd found his master sprawled on the couch in his bedroom and he thought he was dead. But what horrified him the most was the unconscious woman who had clearly been badly beaten and lay bleeding on the floor in Edgar's bedroom. Her hands were bound," Mrs. Cavanaugh swallowed, tears flowing from her eyes. "My husband, Hugh and I rushed to Edgar's house. He wasn't dead as the servant had originally thought. He'd received a shock that rendered him immobile for a long while. After ensuring that the young woman was taken care of, we demanded that Edgar tell us everything. When Edgar saw his brother, he broke down and kept begging for our forgiveness. At first we didn't understand what he was saying because he was quite hysterical and I began to think that my son had gone mad. Then he mentioned the mark on the young woman's shoulder. When Edgar mentioned the mark, I rushed to the room where the poor girl was, checked and saw it. The reason he was begging for Hugh's forgiveness was because he thought he had attacked one of Hugh's daughters. But Hugh assured him that he only had four children and the young woman in the house wasn't one of them. That's when it hit Edgar that the girl could only be his daughter for he knew that he'd sired quite a number himself. The shock of knowing that he'd mercilessly tortured and then nearly defiled his own daughter was too much for Edgar." Mrs. Cavanaugh looked at Amy with so much love and compassion. "That young woman was you and that's how you came to be in our family and in our home. We brought you here to our home so we could take care of you. Your grandfather is really impatient to meet you."

"He didn't touch me?" Amy prayed that it was so.

Mrs. Cavanaugh nodded, quite understanding what her granddaughter was asking. "He'd fully intended to do so but when he tore your gown off and saw the birth mark on your shoulder, he recognized you to be a Cavanaugh, a blood relative. That was like a dash of cold water on his face and it sent him into a reeling shock."

"But how?" Amy remembered that the man she'd seen and who had tormented her was young, not anywhere near her mother's age. "Mama had me when she was in her forties and I'm nineteen," she said. "The man who hurt me looked younger than forty. I don't understand."

"Child, where is your mother and what is her name?"

"Mama died four years ago and her name was Mrs. Chloe Baxter."

Mrs. Cavanaugh scrunched her face as if trying to recall that name but then shook her head. "I don't remember a woman who went by that name working on my estate. All this doesn't make sense but we'll get to the bottom of it." She took a deep breath. "My child, I'm so sorry for what you suffered at the hands of your own father. For all his evil ways, I thank God that Edgar had the honour and sense not to defile his own daughter."

Amy's lips tightened. She would never consider that wicked man as her father. There must be a mistake somewhere because she'd guessed his age to be about thirty six. This meant that he was only about seventeen or eighteen when he sired her. But Amy couldn't imagine her honourable mother being involved with such a young man who'd barely been an adult during her conception. "Where is he now? I don't think I can ever consider him as my father."

"You'll never have to see him again for we buried him five days ago."

"What?" Amy didn't know whether to feel relieved or angry. She'd wanted to know more about how such a scoundrel had convinced her mother and sired her. But the horrible man had died with all the answers to her life and that added to her anger against him.

"When Edgar saw what he'd done to you and realized how close he'd come to committing an abomination by laying with his own daughter, he shot himself. But he begged us to ask you for your forgiveness and when his will was read, he left all his earthly possessions to you including his house, the one...." her grandmother's voice trailed away.

"I want nothing from that evil man," Amy said and started crying.

"Please Amy, you're distraught and I want you to get some rest now. This has been too much for you to take in. When you wake up, I'll be right here."

Amy nodded then something else struck her. "And did you know what kind of business or work he did? How did your son get his wealth?"

"All I found out from his servant was that my son took over a factory which produces matches and he won that in a gambling game. South Something Factory." Amy gave a start but her grandmother didn't notice her white face.. "Edgar was estranged from us and until seven days ago, we hadn't seen him for years. His will mentioned that he left that factory to you as well."

The information was too much for her to take in all at once and she felt like her head was about to explode.

"I want to sleep now."

"Of course, and I'll be right here when you wake up for there's so much that we still need to talk about."

"Yes Ma'am."

"Amy?" Mrs. Cavanaugh's voice dropped to a whisper when she saw Amy drifting off to sleep.

"Yes Ma'am?"

"Would you..." Mrs. Cavanaugh hesitated as if searching for the right words to utter. Amy knew what the other woman wanted to say, felt it in her heart and acknowledged that it was the right thing to do.

"Yes Grandmother, I'm happy to call you that."

"Thank you so much," Mrs. Cavanaugh rose to her feet then bent over and kissed Amy's forehead. "Welcome home, my dear child."

"Thank you, Grandma," she murmured as sleep took over.

11

POT OF GOLD

Brad was really nervous as he paced the floor of the Cavanaugh residence living room. He had no idea how Amy would react to seeing him but he wasn't going to leave until he'd spoken with her and made things right.

He still couldn't believe that he'd found his Amy, or rather Isabelle had.

After leaving Liverpool in anger and with a determination never to return, he'd arrived in London quite broken and in deep despair. Isabelle had berated him all the way and he'd felt quite terrible.

"You shouldn't have convinced me to lie to your family that we were married. And most of all you shouldn't have let Amy believe that. She was deeply hurt."

"Isabelle, I now know that it was a very foolish thing for me to do but other than you finding out if Amy was your relative or not, I needed to know that she still loved me."

"How? By making her think that you'd betrayed her love and married someone else?"

"By seeing if she would be jealous or just dismiss me."

Isabelle gave him an exasperated look. "Honestly Brad, I don't understand the insecurities you men carry around in your heads and hearts."

"Naomi wrote and told me that Amy had found someone else and was about to get engaged to him. I wanted to see for myself if she had stopped loving me," he sighed. "I should have known that Mother was behind it all."

"Don't blame your mother. You too were wrong to wait so long to bring Amy here so she could be with you. And in four years you never once wrote to her or visited so you had no right to test her love in that way. What if she has really found someone else and it's to him that she's now gone? You have lost a woman, who loved you so much, because of your own foolishness. But mostly I blame you for not writing to her, not even once in all the time you were apart."

"I wrote to her several times but she never responded. She never once wrote to me and I began to believe that she didn't care as much as I did."

"Pray tell me, which postal address did you use when you wrote to Amy?"

"The bakery," then is suddenly dawned on him what might have happened. "Mama has always been the one who received letters and she must have intercepted all the ones I wrote to my dear sweet Amy. I'll never forgive her for telling Naomi to write and lie about Amy."

"No family is perfect and I should know," Isabelle said dryly. "I come from a very odd one and have this suspicion that there are many more sisters and brothers out there than Papa will admit to. And Amy must be one of them."

"Where could she have gone? I walked all over Liverpool and even went to the homes of people who I thought might know or have seen her. But no one could tell me where she was. It's like she just dropped off the surface of the earth."

And now here he was about to plead with all that was in him. The door opened and he stopped pacing when he saw Isabelle's grandmother entering the room. He'd met her during Isabelle and Clive's wedding months ago but they didn't speak much at the time. Still, from the look on her face, she recognized him and smiled. Amy was right behind her and when she caught sight of him, turned as if to go back.

"No Child," Everton Cavanaugh was coming in behind her and he gently urged her further into the room.

"What is he doing here?" Amy demanded, heart beating rapidly. She wanted to stare at Brad and see if there were any traces of the love he'd promised on his face but she also wanted to hide from him because her emotions were in turmoil. He was so handsome and in her heart of hearts she knew that she would never love another man the way she loved Brad. He was now a married man which meant he wasn't hers to love anymore and she would eventually find someone else. But she told herself that she would never love again, it hurt too much.

"Listen to him and then act afterwards," was the advice her grandmother gave her. Mrs. Cavanaugh led Amy to a large couch opposite the one Brad was seated on and they sat down side by side. Brad saw the resemblance between Amy and her grandfather who had the same red curly hair and green piercing eyes.

"Talk," Everton barked and Brad felt his palms sweating. It was clear that Amy was well loved; the lost sheep had returned to the fold and the ewe and ram were very protective.

"My name is Brad and your granddaughter Isabelle is my good friend…"

"Your wife you mean," Amy snapped angrily, cutting him off midsentence and before her grandmother could say anything. Why was he even here? Was it to continue tormenting her when she was finally learning to live without him? Her grandparents had embraced her wholly, loving her unconditionally and her heart had just begun to heal.

"Wife?" her grandmother looked at her, then back at Brad. "What's going on here?" Her eyes narrowed. "I know you, didn't we meet months ago?"

"Yes Ma'am, we've met before and I'm here to clear the air about this whole issue. Mrs. Cavanaugh, it was a misunderstanding that I'd like to explain."

"Go on," Mr. Cavanaugh flashed his green eyes at him.

"Clive Fontaine who is Isabelle's husband and I went to school together. When I was done with school, I went to apprentice for my uncle as a lawyer but Clive came looking for me. He'd started a business venture and needed me. So we became partners. I visited their home and met Isabelle and remarked at how closely she resembled someone that I knew because of her thick curly red hair, except for her dark eyes. That's when Isabelle told me about the Cavanaugh Streak which was the birthmark that all who were born of this family possess. She mentioned the green eyes and red curly hair and I remembered that Amy has all those features. We were childhood friends and I remember that other children used to tease her because of the large dark mark on her left shoulder. Her mother told her that she got that mark as a result of being burnt as a child." Brad looked to see if Amy believed his story. Her head was bowed so he couldn't see the expression on her face but went on. At least she hadn't stopped him from speaking. "When I mentioned Amy to Isabelle, she really wanted to see her and asked me to bring Amy to London. But I thought it better that we go to Liverpool and convinced her to accompany me." He fell silent for a moment and the only sound in the room was the shifting logs in the fireplace as they burst into flames.

"It was my idea that we should pose as husband and wife because I needed to know if Amy still loved me or not. Isabelle was against the idea but I convinced her. Only I didn't know that things would turn out so badly."

"You never once wrote to me," Amy wiped her tears away. "You didn't come back like you promised."

"Amy, my darling," Brad forgot that he was in the presence of her grandparents. "I wrote to you so many times but never received any response. It was my mistake that I used the bakery's postal address. I should have used the church one for I'm sure the Vicar would have delivered the letters to you. But I didn't expect that my mother would hide my letters from you. In my last letter I even sent you a postal order for your train ticket so you could come to me in London. I wanted so badly to marry you. But the response I got was from my sister Naomi and she told me that you had met someone else and were in love with him. She even mentioned that the wedding banns would soon be read and that's the reason I came to Liverpool."

"She lied," Amy said earnestly. "I made a promise to wait for you and never once looked at another man."

"I know that now," he shook his head. "When you disappeared, it nearly killed me and I vowed to move heaven and earth to find you. I was in so much pain and anguish that Isabelle feared for my life. Then two days ago, she sent for me and told me that you had been found. Her grandmother had written to her to tell her of your coming to this house."

Amy took a deep breath. "So what now?" She asked.

"I've come to renew my promise to you and to ask your grandparents for your hand in marriage, Amy. I kept my promise to you and never was unfaithful to you, not even once."

Amy shook her head, "You can't want me because I don't know who I am," she whispered tearfully. "The man who sired me is dead and so is my Mama. But I still have so many questions left unanswered and I don't think I can deal with more than that right now."

"Perhaps this might help," Brad reached into his pocket and pulled out a letter. "Before she died, Mrs. Chloe wrote this letter and gave it to my father for safekeeping. She also gave my mother five hundred pounds to use to find your family."

"My family? I don't understand."

"Mrs. Chloe wasn't your birth mother, she told Papa as much. She wanted my father to find your parents and explain everything to them. But Papa had been sickly and unable to travel and kept urging me to come home because he had an urgent matter to discuss with me. If you remember I told you that Clive Fontaine, Isabelle's husband, came looking for me and we became partners," Amy nodded. "We pooled our meagre resources together and bought an old soap factory. Getting it back on its feet so it would begin to turn a profit has been very taxing and we're barely keeping afloat. I couldn't take time off and leave him to run things alone because there were so many problems from mixed up orders by our suppliers to staffing issues. It's been one problem or the other all through so there wasn't ever time for me to take a break and visit home." He sighed. "Amy, I wanted to make you proud and building a strong business is one of the ways in which that was to happen. That's why I wanted you to come to me in London so we could be married since I wasn't able to travel to Liverpool."

"But if your father knew the truth why didn't he tell me?" Amy cried out. "Instead he let me suffer for four years at your mother's hands."

"Amy, nothing I say can make up for the pain that my family caused you and all I can do is ask for your forgiveness and plead for mercy."

Amy leaned into her grandmother's arms and wept. Brad passed the letter to Mr. Cavanaugh who opened the envelope and pulled the sheets of paper out. He cleared his throat.

"Dear Mr. and Mrs. Cavanaugh,

My name is Chloe Baxter and for many years I was one of the midwives who served in Ashton Village where you live. You probably don't know me so I'll explain everything.

I'm writing to you because my sojourn here on earth is coming to an end but I have one who belongs to you.

About sixteen years ago, my daughter Teresa Rider came to work as a housekeeper in your household. Her husband George had been badly injured in an accident at the docks where he worked and was unable to continue providing for his wife and four sons.

Terry was a good girl and she loved her husband very much. You gave her the chance to work and your kindness enabled her to take care of the family where her husband was unable to do so. But George fell seriously ill as a result of the injuries he'd sustained during the accident and the only recourse was an operation to correct what had gone wrong in his body. A lot of money was needed and Terry came to ask you for a loan. But she found out that both of you as well as your eldest son Mr. Hugh had travelled to Paris for your daughter's wedding. Terry met Mr. Edgar Cavanaugh your youngest son who had just come back from school. She pleaded with him for help. He gave her the money alright but took away her dignity and self worth. My daughter had to sell her favours to your seventeen year old son so he would give her the money she needed for her husband's treatment.

When Terry found out that she was with child once more, she came to me. My daughter was broken up because she wasn't sure whether the child was her husband's or Mr. Edgar's"

Amy gave a loud sob and her grandfather paused from reading the letter. Her grandmother's arms tightened around her.

"Please go on," Mrs. Cavanaugh's voice was hoarse and Brad could see the suffering on her face. No mother likes to find out that her child is wicked and manipulative enough to destroy another person's happiness.

"Very well," Mr. Cavanaugh scratched his chin.

"I told Terry to stay calm but when her time drew nigh for her to have her baby, she was to come to me. For nearly nine months we prayed that the child would be a Rider but the Lord had other plans. As soon as I saw the red hair as I was helping deliver my grandchild, then the green eyes and large birth mark on her left shoulder, I knew that the worst had happened. My daughter had given birth to a Cavanaugh. My thirty eight year old daughter had borne a baby for a seventeen year old boy. That would have been the scandal of the century.

Being a midwife it was very easy for me to obtain the corpse of an infant and I found a dark haired little baby boy. I put some herbs in my daughter's food that would make her sleep deeply after she had put to bed. Terry wanted to keep her baby and face the consequences but I knew that doing that would destroy her family. Her husband and sons needed her. So when she was asleep, I put the dead baby by her side and took the beautiful baby girl who I named Amelia Jane Baxter and disappeared out of my children's lives. None of my other children ever found out what had happened because I didn't want Terry shamed. Better that she buried a dead child who everyone believed was her husband's than have to face life with the offspring of a seventeen year old. No one would have believed that Mr. Edgar had manipulated and taken advantage of her desperation. Everyone would have pointed fingers at my child and ridiculed her because Edgar was the same age as her eldest son.

Mr. and Mrs. Cavanaugh, Amy is the daughter of your son Edgar and my prayer is that you'll be merciful to this child because she has no one else. Much as I don't want her mother to ever find out who she is, I know that it's inevitable that they will one day meet. Please keep my granddaughter safe for me.

Please find it in your hearts to forgive me for hiding this truth from you but as parents I know that you would do all you can to protect your children. I was only protecting my child from shame, humiliation and the anguish of having her husband and sons despise her. When the time is right, please tell Amy about her birth parents and if she wants to see her father then so be it. Also, if she asks to see her mother please allow her to do so. Let Amy know that in spite of the mistakes my daughter made, she loved her little girl and was willing to give up everything to keep her.

Please forgive me and I pray that you accept my grandchild into your family. Tell Amy that I loved her even more than I loved my own children because when I left Ashton Village, I never saw or heard from them again. That was so I could protect her.

I remain your humble servant,

Chloe Mary Baxter."

It was a long while before anyone in the room moved or said anything. The letter had stated everything and finally Amy had the answers she sought.

"Grandma," her voice was hoarse from so much weeping.

"My dear Child, I can't begin to understand the anguish you're going through and I'm so sorry. Please forgive my son for his wickedness towards your mother and then to you."

"I wish I could find my mother," Amy said as a fresh flood of tears started. "How she must have felt ashamed and distressed. If it's possible to find her, I'd like to thank her for allowing me to live. She could have done what other women who had been caught up in situations like her have been doing through the ages and had me killed before I saw the light of day. Please Grandma, can you find my mother?"

Brad saw the chance to redeem himself. "Amy, I'll find your mother."

She turned hopeful eyes to him, "Please don't promise me what you can't give me, Brad. I would never forgive you for that."

"It's my promise. Please just give me a few days to find your mother."

"Thank you," she said, giving him a watery smile. Even though it was brief, it was a start and Brad knew he would do everything in his power to find the missing woman and reconcile mother and child. His future happiness and Amy's depended on it.

12

LOVE IS ETERNAL

Amy observed the couple in their forties who looked very nervous. George Rider was gaunt and his wife Teresa fared no better. They had brought their four sons with them and Amy looked on the faces of her half brothers with much compassion. She might have been part of this family that though poor clearly shared deep love. From the way the boys paid attention to their parents, it was obvious that they cared about them.

And she had Brad to thank for finding her family. He'd come through for her and she would forever be grateful to him. But he wasn't part of this meeting now because he had work to do back at the soap factory. Still, he was the one who had brought them in a hired carriage. On his way out, he'd reminded her of the promise he made to her years ago by kissing his right index finger and then placing it on her lips.

That gesture brought back memories both good and bad but she saw it in his eyes that he loved her so much. There was much to forgive and deal with but there was also hope that all would be well.

And now looking at her family she saw the suffering on all their faces. Life had clearly been hard for the Rider family and Amy wiped her eyes. She'd fared no better even though her father had come from wealth. Like her grandmother Chloe had said, Terry had paid a high price for the love she had for her family. Amy knew that if her mother had been given the chance to raise her, she would have been loved by a gentle stepfather and four half brothers. She longed to make herself known to them but her grandparents had told her to be patient.

The silence in the living room stretched for a long while and was finally broken when Terry sank to her knees. Clearly overcome with guilt and fear, she could no longer hold the secrets that she'd kept hidden for nineteen years. No one had told the Riders the reason they'd been brought to this village that they had fled from nineteen years ago but from the way Terry's lips trembled, Amy knew that her mother had an idea.

"Please forgive me," she held her husband's feet and sobbed, placing her head on his lap.

"Terry!"

"Mama!" Andrew the eldest son knelt down and held her in his arms. "It will be alright," he reassured her while frowning at the people he felt were responsible for his mother's distress.

"It's all my fault," Terry said.

Amy was observing George Rider as he looked at his wife. She saw the tender expression on his face and knew that this man truly loved her mother. He'd been a good husband. They were poor yes but they shared a very deep and eternal love.

For days after she'd read her grandmother's letter, she was angry at the way her life had been manipulated. She couldn't understand why her grandmother and mother hadn't given her to the Cavanaughs. But now as she observed her mother and stepfather, she finally understood why Chloe had done what she did those many years ago.

Her maternal grandmother had chosen to preserve a family instead of ripping it apart because of no fault of theirs. A manipulative and wicked man had stepped into the family and turned it upside down and as a loving mother, Chloe had chosen to preserve it at a very great cost.

"George, I wronged you and I'm so sorry," Terry wept.

"My love," George motioned for his son to help his mother back onto the chair. "You've tormented yourself for nineteen years and I prayed that you would trust in the love that I have for you and share your pain with me." He touched her cheek gently. "I know what Edgar Cavanaugh did to you all those years ago."

"You knew?" Terry raised stricken eyes to her husband, hand on her heart. "How?"

"He came to find me just before you stopped working for the Cavanaughs. He was a high spirited seventeen year old and the words he spewed out of his mouth," George shook his head. "I looked at the boy who was the same age as our Andrew and couldn't fathom the depth of wickedness that ran through his heart even at that age. He called me a useless and worthless lout who was sponging off his wife's hard labour. He said you and he were in a relationship and he was the one providing for our family. He also told me that if I was man enough, I should let you go because you were in love with him and even though he was only seventeen, he could take better care of you."

"It was just the one time," Terry bowed her head in shame. "I was so desperate and didn't want you to die."

"I know that and it was so you could get the money for my treatment. Terry, you were a virtuous woman when I married you and I know that many men desired you for themselves but you kept true to me all those years. We shared eighteen years of marriage and I got to know you very well. When Cavanaugh came to see me I was really hurt because of the way he made it seem like you were the one who had pursued him. He said you were with child by him and it nearly broke my heart." George bowed his head as Mrs. Cavanaugh burst into tears. Mr. Cavanaugh had turned as white as a sheet and Amy felt their pain. Her father had destroyed many lives and she just prayed that she would one day find the grace to forgive him. Grandma Chloe had always told her that carrying bitterness destroyed one's own soul. Her father had wanted to destroy her life and if she continued being angry and bitter at him, he would still be having a hold on her life.

Her grandparents had suffered because of their last child's behaviour and hearing how he'd nearly torn a family apart was heartbreaking.

"That young man said the baby you were carrying was a love child and after you had put to bed, he would take you away from me and the boys and prove that he was a better man than I was. Terry, when you returned with a dead dark haired baby, I was so relieved. That boy came to the house with other mourners and I felt that he was really mocking us. But he took one look at the child in the casket and that was the last time I ever saw him." Tears shimmered in his eyes. "Deep down in my heart I knew that the dead baby didn't belong to us and I suspected that your mother had switched babies which meant that you had delivered a child for Edgar Cavanaugh. I saw your pain and anguish every day, my darling. You chose to be poor rather than continue to work in that household and I loved you so much."

"Oh George!"

Mrs. Cavanaugh cleared her throat, wiping her tears. Her husband came over and sat beside her, putting his arm around her.

"We bear the shame for what our son did to you, Mrs. Rider," she said. "I never knew why you had suddenly left our employ because no one ever explained anything to me. Had I known what Edgar did to you, things would have turned out very differently. We are so sorry and beg for your forgiveness."

George and Teresa Rider looked at the wealthy couple disbelief written all over their faces. A heartfelt apology was the last thing they had expected when they were summoned to the manor.

"But that's not the reason we asked you to come," Mrs. Cavanaugh took Amy's hand. "This is the child you gave up, Mrs. Rider. Your mother Mrs. Chloe Baxter took her to Liverpool and that's where they lived all these years. But sadly, your mother passed away four years ago. It was only recently that Amy landed in our hands and we also received a letter from your mother telling us everything that happened nineteen years ago." Mrs. Cavanaugh looked at her husband who gave her a reassuring nod.

Amy and her mother stared at each other for a long time. Everyone present could see the longing in the older woman's eyes and the yearning to hold the only daughter she had ever borne. Amy felt love and compassion well up within her heart for the woman who had paid a very great price for her love for her family. And she remembered what her grandmother had once told her.

"*A mother's love is eternal, child. A loving mother will even walk on hot coals from hell just to protect her family.*"

And that was exactly what had happened to Terry. Edgar Cavanaugh had made her walk on hot coals from hell for nineteen years. He'd taken advantage of a desperate woman and wrecked her life and happiness for a long time.

Amy rose to her feet and approached her mother. She fell to her knees before her and placed her head on her lap.

"My baby," Terry's voice broke as she placed a hesitant hand on Amy's head, stroking her hair gently. "My beautiful daughter." Then Amy hugged her mother for the very first time and the two of them wept in each other's arms for a long while.

Years of pain, rejection and abuse rolled away as mother and daughter found acceptance and peace that had eluded them for so long. There wasn't a dry tear in the room.

Amy finally raised her head and looked at her stepfather who was observing the two of them with tears running down his cheeks.

"Will you allow me to call you Papa?" she approached him while still on her knees. "You would have been such a good father to me, I know."

"Oh Child," George's voice was hoarse. He held out his arms and she accepted his embrace, feeling his strong heart even though his body was frail. "It's true, I would have loved you like I do your brothers."

13

IT ALL ENDS WELL

SIX MONTHS LATER

"**A**re you sure you know what you're doing, Amy?" Clive Fontaine asked her.

"Yes. The soap factory though small is doing very well and that other place reminds me of the very pits of hell. It's not just a match factory but has been used as a front for a brothel. Desperate women like I once was go there hoping to find jobs to take care of their families but end up being sold to men who abuse them and take their self worth and dignity from them. I was lucky to have escaped but what about the countless number of women who had no one to defend them? How many lives did that man and his cronies destroy?" Tears were falling from her eyes. "Who will ever restore the dignity of those poor women?"

"My love," Brad placed a gentle hand on her arm. "Clive and I will do everything to make sure that all those who were involved in those terrible deeds face the full wrath of the law. Meanwhile, we'll look over the books and do a complete overhaul of the factory. If it's doing well then we can continue with production of matches because they're needed in every household. We'll change the production process so it isn't risky to the health of the women and men who work there. But if the books show losses then you can go ahead and change the business."

But Amy shook her head. "I would rather shut that place and even burn it down to the ground than let those women suffer any more. Soap production is much safer than matches. I know that I'm still new at everything but I care about what happens to those women who work in my factory. I've spoken to a number of those who pack the matches and they highlighted the effects of all those chemicals on their health. I won't have that on my conscience. Others may think that making a profit is important but not to me. If you don't think soap manufacturing is ideal then I would rather make thread or even textiles. But no more matches and I expect the changes to take place immediately."

"But what happens to the workers during the transition? We may have to shut down for a few days or weeks as we overhaul the whole system. That means loss of earnings for those who need them desperately."

Amy smiled, "My grandparents are my trustees. Much as I never wanted to touch any of the money or property that man left me, I'm doing it for the many women he abused over the years, including my mother. Let that money do some good. My grandparents confirmed with Mr. Edgar's lawyers that he left me vast wealth. Even though he was a wicked man in other ways, when it came to business ventures he was very shrewd and amassed a large amount of money and properties. That is the money that will sustain the wages of all the workers in my factory until it begins operations again and can make a profit. Better yet, why not let your factory take it over completely and the two of you can run it. I'll be a silent partner in all this. I have the means and will to do it so the rest is up to the two of you." She turned to Brad. "My grandparents would like us to sit down so that we can go over all the documents and I told them that I would be selling off many of the properties so I can improve the factory and working conditions of those in my employ."

"Very well then," Clive said. "We're on board with your ideas, Ma'am."

"Oh Clive," Amy giggled. "I'm still just Amy."

Brad wondered why the lights in the house were on even though he was sure he'd switched them off that morning as they were leaving for the factory. Since both of them were hardly at home, they didn't have full time staff. A cleaning woman came in twice a week to do the laundry and clean the house but Amy insisted on cooking for her husband.

Then he remembered that today was the day Sarah Carver their housekeeper came by the house. She must have turned the lights on and then forgotten to turn them off when she was leaving.

He remarked as much to his wife as he opened the front door and ushered her in. But she just gave him a loving smile as they entered the house and locked the door, saying nothing about the lights that were burning in the living room.

"Amy, my darling," he helped her take her coat off. "I'm so proud of you and for the woman you've

149

become. In such a short time you have shown your compassion and turned things around for so many women." He held her by the shoulders and looked deep into her eyes. "I nearly lost you and it makes me tremble inside."

"Sh!" She slipped her arms around his waist and hugged him tight. "But you didn't and I want us to be happy and not keep crying about the past. It's gone and we've received grace for a new future, a better one."

"I can never forget what my family did to you and for as long as I live, I'll continue begging you for mercy for them."

"Which is why," she opened the door leading to the living room and Brad who was following her came to a sudden stop. His parents and sisters were standing in the room looking at him with fear in their eyes. "I asked my brother Derek to travel to Liverpool and bring your family here without telling them the truth. He told them that you were very ill and had sent for them to come so they didn't hesitate in making the journey to London." She turned to the Pikes. "Mr. and Mrs. Pikes, you took me in after my grandmother died and even though things weren't good, I'm choosing to forgive and let go because I love your son, who is my husband, very much. He's the only man I have ever loved and now that we're going to have a baby, we want you to be part of our family. A child needs his or her grandparents and my own life has changed so much ever since I met my paternal grandparents six months ago."

Mrs. Pikes broke down and kept repeating how sorry she was. Naomi and May were weeping and their father had his arms around their shoulders. It took Brad and Amy a long while to calm the distraught women down but eventually they fell silent.

"This is beyond what I prayed for, Mr. Pikes said. "I never knew that a day like this one would ever come, not after what we did to you, Amy. Thank you for forgiving us."

Amy smiled at him. "I also ask for your forgiveness because I know that I wasn't the easiest person to live with."

"Pa, Amy and I would like for you to sell the bakery and house in Liverpool and come to London. We've bought a property on Euston Square which will be ideal for a new bakery since it's close to Euston

Railway Terminal and that means big business for you."

$$\sim$$

"Belinda Taylor where are you?" the supervisor called out. "Belinda, can you step forward please?"

A dishevelled woman stepped out from the crowd and trudged forward. She looked exhausted and Amy's heart nearly broke at the hopelessness etched on her friend's face. This was supposed to be a Christian Workhouse but the conditions here were deplorable and Amy felt angry that people who were supposed to show love and compassion were instead abusing desperate people.

Belinda was heavily pregnant but determined to stay strong. After the mysterious disappearance of her friend from the match factory, she'd tried to search for her. When rumours started flying around that Amy's body had been fished from the Thames, Belinda wanted answers. No one had any explanation as to how that had happened and when Belinda persisted in her quest for the truth, was dismissed from her employ.

She'd only been paid wages twice and she had trudged through the streets of London for days without food and sleeping at Euston Railway Station which was always busy day and night.

One day hunger drove her to beg a food vendor for something to eat and the woman raised a cry calling her a thief. She was lucky not to have been lynched because two police constables were taking lunch at the same café. They hauled her down to the precinct and because of her advanced pregnancy didn't toss her into prison. Instead they put her in this workhouse.

"Belinda," Amy could no longer hold back but rushed towards her friend who stepped back in slight alarm. "Don't be afraid, it's me Amy Baxter. I've been searching all over for you. It's taken me nearly six months to find you because when I went back to the match factory they told me you had left."

"Amy, is it really you?" Belinda touched her expensive coat and looked at her in wonder. "I was told that you had died. The body of a young woman was fished from River Thames and we were told that it was you."

Amy was laughing and crying at the same time. "A lot has happened in the past six months that I don't know where to begin. But God spared my life because I nearly died. It's a long story but enough of that for now." Even though Belinda was scruffy looking and Amy was dressed smartly, the two women hugged each other. "I've come to take you home with me."

"You look so different, Amy," and then she looked over her friend's shoulder and noticed the two gentlemen standing quietly on one side. "Bradford Pikes, is that you?"

Belinda's face showed her astonishment. "I must be dreaming."

Brad chuckled softly as he stepped forward. "You're not dreaming dear girl, it's really me. And this," he pointed at the other man, "Is my brother-in-law, Derek Rider. He's Amy's brother."

Amy noticed that Derek couldn't seem to take his eyes off Belinda and smiled inwardly. His eyes were shining as if he'd suddenly discovered a stash of precious jewels among the rubble and when he shook her hand, held on for longer than necessary. Amy saw that her brother was smitten by her friend and was seeing beyond her current state of dressing. She would do all she could to make sure that the two of them ended up falling in love.

Life had turned around for her after so many years of pain and she wanted to give back as much as she could to others.

"Amy my darling, you can't save the whole world or solve everyone's problems," her husband told her a few days later when he found out that she was looking to donate a good amount of money to a women's shelter that also catered to abandoned children.

"I know that but every single penny counts. I'm realistic and a dreamer at the same time," she snuggled closer to him, letting the warmth from his large body engulf her.

"And I love you so much for what you're doing to alleviate other people's pain but I don't want you to over tax yourself."

"Brad, it frightens me that there could be other children out there sired by Edgar Cavanaugh. I do all I can to help the orphans and needy and pray that if my father sired other children, someone is taking care of them until we can find them and bring them back home."

"You're a very noble woman."

"And I'm lucky to have you in my life. You're the one who has given me the strength to do all this, Brad. Your love, support and counsel are my strength."

"No my dear, all that is the Lord's doing. I'm just but His vessel but I'll always be here for you."

"Mr. Bradford Pikes, do you know how much I love you?" She whispered, giving him a look that warmed his heart.

"I have an inkling and I want you to know that you're treasured, loved and for as long as there's breath in my body, I'll be loving you, Amelia Jane Pikes."

As they listened to the sounds of the night outside their window, they both knew that they were blessed. It had been a long journey but they were finally home.

THANK YOU FOR CHOOSING A PUREREAD BOOK!

We hope you enjoyed the story, and as a way to thank you for choosing PureRead we'd like to send you this free book, and other fun reader rewards…

Click here for your free copy of Whitechapel Waif
PureRead.com/victorian

Thanks again for reading.
See you soon!

OUR GIFT TO YOU

AS A WAY TO SAY THANK YOU WE WOULD
LOVE TO SEND YOU THIS BEAUTIFUL
STORY FREE OF CHARGE.

Our Reader List is 100% FREE

Click here for your free copy of Whitechapel Waif

PureRead.com/victorian

At PureRead we publish books you can trust. Great tales
without smut or swearing, but with all of the mystery and
romance you expect from a great story.

Be the first to know when we release new books, take part
in our fun competitions, and get surprise free books in

your inbox by signing up to our Reader list.

As a thank you you'll receive an exclusive copy of Whitechapel Waif - a beautiful book available only to our subscribers...

Click here for your free copy of Whitechapel Waif

PureRead.com/victorian